It's My Life

I knew something was wrong as soon as I stepped into the hall. The trouble was, I didn't know how I knew. If there had been obvious signs—anything unusual, any sound, anything at all—I would have turned round and walked straight out again.

But Martin doesn't walk out again and within minutes he finds himself in the middle of a nightmare. He is kidnapped and held captive on a canal boat—but that is only the beginning. When Martin finds out who his kidnapper is, and who he is in league with, the horror deepens and Martin has to use all his ingenuity to escape—with Hannah's help.

MICHAEL HARRISON was born in Oxford in 1939. He has taught in North Queensland, London, Oxford, and Hartlepool but is now a part-time librarian in Oxford and enjoys visiting schools as a writer. He is married and has two grown-up sons. His previous books include a history of witches, funny novels, retellings of Norse myths, a book of poems, *Junk Mail*, and a retelling of *Don Quixote*.

It's My Life

OTHER OXFORD BOOKS BY MICHAEL HARRISON

Junk Mail

Don Quixote

It's My Life

Michael Harrison

Oxford University Press
Oxford New York Toronto

Oxford University Press, Great Clarendon Street,
Oxford OX2 6DP

Oxford New York
Athens Auckland Bangkok Bogota Bombay
Buenos Aires Calcutta Cape Town Dar es Salaam
Delhi Florence Hong Kong Istanbul Karachi
Kuala Lumpur Madras Madrid Melbourne
Mexico City Nairobi Paris Singapore
Taipei Tokyo Toronto

and associated companies in
Berlin Ibadan

Oxford is a trade mark of Oxford University Press

First published 1997

A CIP catalogue record for this book is available
from the British Library

ISBN 0 19 271749 9

Cover design and illustration by Slatter Anderson

Printed and bound in Great Britain by
Biddles Ltd, Guildford and King's Lynn

This book is for Mary and John

1
Tuesday 18 December 3.35 p.m.
Martin . . .

I knew something was wrong as soon as I stepped into the hall. The trouble was, I didn't know *how* I knew. If there had been obvious signs—anything unusual, any sound, anything at all—I would have turned round and walked straight out again. I stood in the hall, one hand still on the door handle, the door still open behind me. I looked round. Everything was in its right place, including me.

I had been in such trouble last night that I didn't dare not be in the right place. INSIDE THE HOUSE BY TWENTY-FIVE TO FOUR. Those were my instructions. School finished at 3.15. I was allowed five minutes to gather my belongings together and fifteen minutes to walk home. Mum had been so angry yesterday that she had gone straight out and walked to school to find out how long it took. I had to be in my house. I was not allowed to go to any of my friends' houses. I was certainly not allowed to go to the shops again. If she rang up—when she rang up—I had to be here to answer. Or else.

I had an exact time to get home. I had got home on time, early in fact because I had hung around talking, just to prove I didn't care, wasn't bothered. I had then been so worried I might be late, might not be in for the phone call, that I had run some of the way. Now I was here, panting slightly in the doorway, but on time. But this was just the start. I had an exact timetable for when I was back. It was stuck to the fridge door with a magnet in the shape of a chocolate bar. A chocolate bar! Anything else would have been better: chains for example. They would be more suitable for a prison-house.

I was the prisoner. I was also the prison warden. The prison was guarded by telephone, and by fear of the 'or else'.

So, 3.35 and I was standing inside the hall and something was wrong.

'Hello!' I called.

There was no answer. The silence began to get to me. That was one reason I had got into trouble yesterday. I really didn't like walking into the house when no one was there, especially at this time of year when it got dark early. But I couldn't say so, could I? Mum kept going on about how I was a big boy now, the man of the house. She kept going on about how hard she had to work to keep me, how little money my dad gave her. How could I stand there and say I was too frightened to walk into my own house, was frightened of the silence?

It wasn't even the silence. It was the nearly silence. If you stood in the hall, like I was standing at that moment, and listened, you heard noises. A lot of them came from the road outside but when you shut the door there were still little sounds. If you are in a house by yourself there are always little sounds all around you. Probably safe sounds. But how do you know? I had tracked them round the house until I knew each one. It was worse in winter because the heating going on and off made a whole lot of different noises. I had taught myself to recognize them so that I knew now exactly what happened. Sometimes I thought it was best to put the TV on to drown out all the little noises and sometimes I thought it was best to be able to hear if someone was creeping up on me. I didn't like stepping into the empty house. I didn't like being in the house by myself. I would have liked to have been able to go round to a friend's house, but I wasn't allowed. I wasn't really allowed friends. And today I had orders. Today I had a timetable. Today I was going to have to listen to the little sounds.

No TV today. It wasn't on my timetable. Next was 3.40: A DRINK AND A BISCUIT. I shut the front door, hung up my coat tidily and walked into the kitchen.

I checked the time on the clock on the cooker: 3.37 it said. I had three minutes still in hand. Perhaps I should use those minutes to check the list of instructions on the fridge. I wouldn't have time later:

MARTIN
3.35: Get home
3.40: drink and a biscuit
3.45: do your homework
4.15: tidy your room
4.30: peel 4 potatoes

That's my life, I thought bitterly.

I opened the fridge and took out a bottle of milk and poured myself a mug. As I put the bottle back in the fridge the motor came on; another of the regular noises, and one of the friendlier ones. I went to the cupboard and took out the biscuit tin. Mum had probably counted them this morning so I'd better just have one, as instructed. She had been in a foul mood at breakfast, complaining about me, about the state of my room, and about having a headache. I put my one biscuit in my mouth as the phone started to ring.

The phone starting to ring always makes me jump; there's no warning, just this sudden scream. It's worse than a baby: 'Pick me up! Pick me up!' it yells through the house. I'd been expecting this call, the Secret Police checking up on me, but it still made me jump. I hadn't really got time to jump. She'd probably timed how long it would take me to walk from the biscuit tin to the phone so I walked briskly to it.

I put the last piece of biscuit in my mouth so that she would hear that I had so far followed instructions to the letter and put my hand out to pick up the phone which was nagging away at me still.

A hand came down on mine and held it down on the phone.

Another hand came over my mouth at the same moment. The phone rang and rang, crying out for attention, crying out in what Mum must have thought was an empty house. Every muscle of mine seized up. I thought I had stopped breathing. I thought my heart had stopped beating.

I was looking down at this hand on top of mine. It looked black and shiny like something that has crawled out of a swamp but it wasn't slimy on my hand. It was warm, and smooth and, strangely, almost comforting, like having your hand held always is. All I could hear was the phone shrieking. All I could feel was the warm weight of the glove pressing my hand down. It was as if my hand was crying, crying, and this gloved hand was comforting it.

The phone stopped suddenly, in mid cry. The silence was huge and filled the hall. I tried to open my mouth to breathe, why did I need to open my mouth, my mouth full of soggy biscuit? I realized somehow for the first time that a glove was squeezing my mouth shut. I realized it must belong to the other hand because I could feel a body behind me. Now everything rushed at me suddenly. The hall leapt at me. Panic ran along every vein in my body. It clung to my hair and pulled it. It danced in my stomach. It roared in my ears. It leaked out of my eyes and trickled down my leg.

'It's all right,' a voice said quietly behind my ear. 'Just be still. Be quiet.'

The hand moved from the telephone. It reached out to the coats that hung up by the front door. It lifted up Mum's blue mac. It dropped it over my head so that the world suddenly disappeared. I was inside a stuffy black cave. The voice spoke again.

'If you scream I'll gag you, tie your mouth up. You won't like that.'

The glove moved cautiously away from my mouth. I took in a great gulp of the stuffy black air. The glove instantly clamped its shiny self round my mouth again. I could taste my own saliva, cold on the glove.

'Do you want to be gagged?'

I shook my head. The glove moved again. I breathed in slowly, cautiously, as if I was stealing the air.

'That's better,' the voice said. 'Do exactly what you're told and you won't be hurt. Now, we're going to walk into the kitchen, slowly.'

One hand gripped my shoulder, hard, holding the mac down on it. I could feel the tension of the cloth pulling on my head. It was pulled towards me so that I couldn't see past it down to my feet. The hand pushed firmly. I took small paces, feeling where I was going. I put my hand out to find the doorway but my arm was slapped down sharply. The hand on my shoulder gripped and pushed.

'Where's the string?' the voice said. The man could obviously see it was a kitchen where everything had its place. My mug of milk was the only thing not where it should be. And me. I shouldn't be in the kitchen. I should be doing homework in my room.

I tried to speak but my voice choked. The hand shook me. I cleared my throat. 'Second drawer down.'

I was pushed a bit further. Held still. I heard the drawer being opened.

'Scissors?'

'Top drawer.'

I heard that being opened. I was pushed further, to my left. I was turned round, pushed back. I could feel the chocolate-bar magnet pressing into my shoulder. My back was to the fridge door. Its motor was silent now.

'Hold out your left hand.'

I held it out. String was tied round my wrist. The knot was pulled tight with his fingers between the string and my wrist so that it wasn't too tight.

'Now your right.' I held out my right wrist. Today I had to obey orders. Today, people had decided to order me around, efficient, organized people.

The same piece of string went round that wrist. It was pulled until my hands were touching and then it was tied in the same careful way. The string was pulled, moving my hands like a reluctant dog. The mac wasn't being held round my face now and I could see straight down and could breathe more easily. The string was being tied round the fridge door handle.

The man tugged hard at the knots and grunted. My brain had begun to unfreeze now. I thought of all the things people did on TV to escape from these situations.

'Try anything and I'll smash you,' the man said, as if he could see into my head. I looked down and twisted my hands so that I could see what time it was. I needed to do something and it was all I could think of. I stared at my watch but it didn't make any sense to me.

'Right,' the man said, 'you stay there nice and quiet and you'll be all right.'

I heard him walk away from me to the kitchen door. There was a pause, as if he was watching me. I stood still and breathed as quietly as I could in case he thought I was drawing breath to scream. There wasn't any point in screaming. There was no one to hear and he probably really would smash me. Why shouldn't he? And I didn't feel like screaming. I felt like becoming really small and invisible.

I heard the creak of the third stair and I knew where he was. I listened hard and heard a door being opened quietly. I couldn't tell which it was but it was upstairs. Knowing where he was, knowing he wasn't watching me, knowing he wasn't about to smash me made me feel better. I leant forwards and tugged at the mac and felt it pull up over my head and then it fell with a rush to the floor. Light dazzled me.

I stood still and listened. There were faint noises from

upstairs, drawers being opened perhaps. I looked all round me, looked at Mum's tidy kitchen. It was not quite so tidy now: my mug, a ball of string, a pair of scissors—all out of place, and all out of reach. I was tied to the fridge door with about ten centimetres of string between me and the handle. I couldn't reach anything except my timetable which sat on the white fridge door and glared at me. It would soon be time for me to tidy my room. It would be worse now because it sounded as though the man was untidying everything upstairs.

I looked at the knots. The ones on my wrists were out of reach because of the way my hands had been tied. I could reach the ones on the fridge handle but it was pointless. I did try to untie them. I had felt him tugging at them when he tied them and they were biting into each other like the worst shoe-lace tangle. The fridge magnet was sensible safe plastic with a little round magnet stuck on to it. There was no way I could use it to saw through the string like they would in a film. I stood there helplessly.

Then I realized: fridge doors open. I opened it cautiously. It gave that little sucking noise as the rubber seal came away from the main body. It sounded very loud to me. I hoped he hadn't heard it up there. I pulled it open as wide as it would go. Mum would shout at me if she was here: letting all the cold air out. I was now by the work-surface that ran between the fridge and the sink. The scissors were by the sink, still out of reach. Think! I urged myself. I tried to remember all the films I'd seen on TV, all the ways of escaping when you're tied up. Then I realized again. My mind seemed to work in jumps at the moment.

There was no way that my hands could reach the scissors, but my feet could. I turned to face the work-surface and put my hands on it. I jumped myself up, sort of pivoting on my hands and turning on to my front, pressing down with my elbow as I landed to stop myself sliding off again. I lay on my stomach, hands stretched out towards the fridge door and eased my feet along, gently, so gently. I could see the scissors in my mind, I could see them clattering into the sink, I could see the man rushing in, grabbing them, sticking them into my defenceless back . . .

I lay very still for a moment, listening. There was no pounding on the stairs, just the occasional quiet noises of someone searching. I stretched out my feet, slowly, slowly.

My trainer touched the scissors. I pressed down with my toe, tried to pull them towards me. They wouldn't move the way I wanted. They tried to slip further away. It took me a moment to realize it was impossible. Lying on my stomach I couldn't move my foot towards me along the work-surface. My foot would only come towards me through the air. I slid my whole body along until my head was pushing against the wall. I took my trainer off the scissors and carefully slid back as far as I could but they were still out of reach of course, because I couldn't move my hands far from the fridge door. I lifted my head and looked down. Mum's mac was lying on the floor below the work-surface. If I flicked the scissors off they would land on the mac, should land on the mac. If I missed they would be out of my reach for good and the clatter would call the man. Risk it! I said to myself. Go on, I said to myself, risk it!

I flicked my foot sideways and felt the scissors jump off. I heard by the sound they made landing that they'd fallen on to cloth and not on to the kitchen tiles. I twisted over and slipped down silently so that I was standing on the floor again and pulled the mac towards me with my foot. I twisted it round until the scissors lay at my feet.

At my feet. Still at my feet! They were completely out of reach of my hands. I was no further forward. At each stage I had a brilliant idea but each brilliant idea just led me up a new dead end. The man would come down soon, see what I had done, and smash me. Perhaps he'd have to kill me because I'd see his face and would be able to describe him and pick him out in an identity parade. I began to panic. I'd be a dead end soon. The fridge motor started up again, sounding very loud. I pushed the door shut, dragging the mac after me.

I had to do something to stop the panic rising, rising; I had to do something, anything, rather than stand there getting more and more worked up. In desperation I pushed my right trainer off with my left foot. I pushed away at my sock, pushing it down my ankle. I stood on the toe and pulled. With a jerk, the sock came off. I wedged my big toe through one finger hole of the scissors and carefully lifted my foot, twisting my knee to bring my foot right up. My fingers closed round the blades. Yes!

I cut through the string that held me to the fridge and then cut the string between my hands. I slipped my foot back into my trainer and the scissors into my pocket and stood and thought. Back door? Front door? Think!

Back door: out into the garden, over the fence, no one at home either side. Who would be in down the road? How long would it be before he caught me scrambling over the fence? Grabbed my ankle and scraped me off the fence? Would I get as far as the fence? Key to put in the lock. No, key to take off its hook and put in the lock and turn. Bolt to slide back. Noise. Time.

Front door: out and away down the road, people . . . but across the hall. He could be coming down the stairs, could leap down and grab me and . . .

The phone rang. Its sudden hysterical cry making me jump and run towards it. Mum.

'Mum!' I shouted as I picked the phone up. 'Mum! Help! There's a man here. He tied me up. Quick!'

There was a voice on the phone, not Mum's voice. 'Janet,' it was saying, 'is that you, dear? What's going on? Who's that shouting? Don't say I've got a wrong number again. Oh, this phone!'

'Help me!' I yelled, but the phone just purred at me.

All this time there had been more sounds, banging, running, and now jumping down stairs. I had had my back turned while I was speaking, facing the phone, facing Mum, I thought, hiding from everything else. I put the phone down carefully, thinking it was important that Mum could ring and then I turned, just as the man lost his balance rushing down the stairs and fell forward on to his face, sliding the last two steps and sprawling by the front door.

Front door: blocked. Back door: too slow. Stairs: blocked. Help! Why wasn't my dad here to look after me? Then I remembered and ran across the hall, pulled open the door to the cupboard under the stairs, crammed myself in, squirmed half round again, pulled the door shut, and pushed the bolt in. I sat, panting, remembering.

Mum and Dad had had one of their biggest rows ever in front of me over that bolt. I'd been nagging Dad, on and on, wanting a tree-house. I don't remember now why it was so important for me to have a tree-house but I remember it was the only thing I thought about for weeks. I couldn't have one. We didn't have a proper tree in our garden but I was too young to realize this. I thought Dad could grow one, or plant one, or build a tree-house somewhere else. In the end he put a bolt on the inside of the cupboard door. 'That's an inside-a-tree-house,' he said. It was great in there when I was small, squeezing in behind the Hoover and all the stuff that fills cupboards to the far end where the stairs meet the floor and I could really imagine I was living inside a tree. It was the sort of brilliant thing Dad thought of. Mum really went for him. Not safe, she said. I'd lock myself in. The bolt would stick. On and on and on. Taking away all the pleasure I had had, all the pleasure I had shared with Dad. I never went in there again after that row, until now.

I couldn't see anything, but you could hear quite a lot in there. I heard the man swearing. He came across to the cupboard and pulled at the door, expecting it to open. He swore again, kicked it.

'Open this door,' he shouted. 'Open it, or I'll smash it in and you with it, you little . . .'

I squirmed away from the door, round the Hoover, but couldn't get very far. There was more junk in the cupboard now, and I was much bigger. He kicked the door a couple of times and then just stood there. I could hear him breathing through the wood. Then it went quiet.

I felt around me, feeling everything and trying to remember what was in the cupboard, what might be useful. I managed to get the scissors out of my pocket. They might make him hold back a bit. Very soon, though, there were more noises, scraping and a bump against the door.

'If you won't come out, you can stay in till I'm ready for you,' the man's voice came. 'You won't move that in a hurry.'

His feet went over my head up the stairs, thumping down as if they would break through at any moment and land on me: thump! Thump! There was the ghost of an echo sighing down the stairs. Then silence. In the silence the noise from outside seemed louder for a moment. Then silence, nothing. There was a little edge of light round the door, enough to see where it was but not enough to see anything. I was in the muffled dark. I needed the toilet.

As I sat there in the dark, desperate for what Mum insisted I call 'the loo', I began to panic about air. It seemed to me that it was running out. I tried to breathe slowly but found I was panting. Panic came out of the dark and attacked again. It wasn't so bad when I was moving, doing something, just planning something even, but I couldn't just sit. It was like playing hide-and-seek when you can't bear not to peep and see if they're coming to look for you. I think I was safe locked in, wedged in, but I didn't feel safe. I didn't know what the man was doing, where he was. Suppose he set fire to the house to destroy the evidence and the witness? I listened for the crackling of furniture, sniffed for the smoke that would sidle under the door, sneak down my throat in the dark, fill my lungs . . . Why didn't we have a smoke detector like all my friends?

I moved quietly back to the door. I slid the bolt, slowly, carefully, silently. He might be there, waiting, his trap set. There might be nothing wedging the door closed. I would heave at it and fall out, straight into his hands. I moved the bolt back again and sat listening. There was no sound of breathing on the other side of the door; there was no sound at all.

I eased the bolt. I very lightly pushed the door. It moved about a centimetre, stopped. Something was holding it. I put my mouth to the crack and gulped at the air outside. I pushed a little harder. Nothing happened. I put the scissors down and turned round so that my back was to the door, wedged my feet against the Hoover, and pushed. There was a scraping sound as the door moved another centimetre or two, then stopped. The noise frightened me and I held on to the door, ready to pull it shut again. Nothing.

I knelt up and eased the door open. My fingers just edged through the gap. I bent them round and felt with my finger-tips. Soft: cloth: a chair. I felt down and felt the smooth wooden leg of the chair Mum always sat in to watch TV. I ought to be able to push that. But if I pushed it, it would make that scraping noise, it might topple over, crash on to the floor. The man would run down the stairs again, run more carefully this time. I must plan exactly what to do.

I shut my eyes and pictured the hall. Pictured where the chair would be when the door was open enough for me to slip out. Pictured the lock on the front door—that was my only escape route in the time I would have. Planned out every step in my head.

I wedged my feet against the Hoover again and put my shoulder to the door. I took a deep breath and pushed as hard as I could. Nothing happened for a moment and then it all happened at once. Whatever was holding the chair in place suddenly gave way. The chair slid across the floor. The door swung open and I fell forward on to my hands like one of those sprinters you see on TV.

2
Tuesday: 3.55 approximately
Martin

A hand held my ankle. I tried to get up but the hand jerked my leg and I fell over again. The voice said, 'I keep telling you: do what you're told and you won't get hurt. Do you think I want to hurt you? Don't make me, just don't make me hurt you.' The hand let go of my ankle and grasped my arm. I was pulled to my feet and pushed back into the kitchen. Mum would not be pleased. Her mac was lying on the floor with some bits of string. Two drawers were open. There was a dirty sock. There was a mug half full of milk. There was me. There was the man.

He pushed me back towards the fridge. He bent down and picked up Mum's mac and dropped it back over my head so that the world disappeared again. Somehow I didn't feel frightened now. I knew what was going to happen. He was going to tie me to the fridge again and take the scissors away. I would have to stay there until Mum came home. I could manage that. It shouldn't be too long now, about an hour. I could manage an hour.

'I'm going to tell you what we're going to do,' the voice came. 'Just listen and if you do exactly what I say, you'll be fine and it will all end happily ever after. We've got two things to do. First, we are going to leave a message for your mother so that she knows what's going on. I'm going to sit you at the table so that you can write and you'll write what I tell you.'

While he was saying this he pushed me quite gently until I could feel my knees against the side of a chair. He turned me and I sat down. He pulled the coat forward so that I could see the table. He pushed a piece of paper in front of me and then a pencil. I recognized them. They had been in my room, waiting for me to do my homework. I knew the pencil well. It had been sharpened until about half was left. It had my tooth marks pitting the yellow paint so that it was flaking off at the end. It lay there now on the piece of paper, like a traitor. I didn't want to pick it up.

'Pick up the pencil,' the voice said, 'and write this.' Slowly I picked it up. Its feel in my hand brought back the safety of my room, the safe boredom of homework, of the sound of Mum downstairs getting supper ready. A tear dropped on to the piece of paper, spread out. Another followed. I sniffed, blinked, tried to hold it in. Boys don't cry, do they? I made myself remember how much I hated being made to stay in my room by myself between school and supper. Cosy family life wasn't something I'd had much of lately. Why cry, then?

'Write this: "Dear . . ." and then put whatever you call her. OK? "I am all right. I am not hurt. I have been kidnapped"—two p's—"and you will receive more instructions later. Do not"—underline not—"tell the police, or else." Now sign it.'

I wrote 'Martin'.

A hand in its glove came under the mac and picked up the paper. I held on to the pencil and then slipped it into my pocket. I could feel it pressing against my leg, a comforting pressure. The man spoke again.

'We'll leave this on the fridge door where she'll see it. Now, this is the tricky bit. I've got to get you out of here without anyone noticing. It's up to you. You co-operate and you won't get hurt and we can get all this sorted out very quickly and you'll be home and safe and it will all be over. That's one choice. The other choice you have is to try to get away or attract attention. You might succeed. You might get away. If you do, I might too. And I'd come after you again. You'd never feel safe, would you? Any time you opened a door, I might be behind it. Any corner you go round, I might be waiting. That's if you're lucky and get away. If you're unlucky and don't get away . . . well, I'm going to get pretty annoyed, aren't I? I'm not going to be able to trust you. You might get seriously hurt and you'd definitely have a pretty uncomfortable time. It's a bit of a lottery, isn't it? And I don't think you've got much chance of winning.'

'I'll be quiet,' I said.

'You'd have to say that. I don't know whether you're telling me the truth or not so I'll not be able to trust you. Just remember that.'

I felt the mac being pulled off my head. Light didn't flood in as it had before. It was already getting dark outside. The man was standing behind me. I didn't turn my head to look at him. It would be best to let him think I wasn't going to try to escape, and then it could be easy to slip away in the dark. I'd need to get a good look at him so that I could tell the police. But I'd wait, pretend.

'I'm going to tie a piece of string round your wrist so that I can hold the other end. We're going to walk out, shutting the door carefully behind us. We will walk along the road and down to the canal. If you see anyone you know you'll smile nicely at them but say nothing and keep walking. Remember: your best bet is to do exactly what you're told.'

He lifted my left arm and put it on the table. He tied a loop of string round my wrist, just as he had before. Being tied up again made me feel how hopeless it was to try to escape. Everything I'd done, all the panic and all the feeling of outwitting him, had come to exactly nothing. Perhaps he was right. How could I beat a ruthless adult who had planned this all out? But why kidnap me? Why?

He finished tying the string round my wrist and gave it a tug to make sure it wouldn't slip over my hand. 'Get your coat,' he said.

I walked to the front door, to where I had hung my

coat when I came in from school, so long ago it seemed now. I put it on facing the wall and then slowly turned. I don't know quite what I expected to see, some sort of monster I suppose. What I did see surprised me, it was so normal. He was just a man in the kitchen doorway, about the same height as most people, at least I couldn't say he was especially tall or especially short. He had a dark grey coat on, with the collar turned up and a scarf round his neck, rather pulled up round his face, and one of those flat caps, pulled down at the front. There wasn't much of his face showing through all this: a nose stuck out but that looked normal too.

He took one step towards me and bent down and picked up a blue bag from the bottom of the stairs. It was my bag. It was the one I used when I went to stay with Dad for the weekend. Why couldn't Dad be here to sort everything out? Seeing the bag made it all much worse somehow. It was bad enough that he'd come to burgle our house, but to take my bag! He should have brought his own bag to put the valuables in, but he'd have been disappointed in our house; there weren't any valuables. Perhaps that was why he was kidnapping me. I remembered something we'd done in history at school. Morton's Fork, it was called. In the old days the tax collectors came round and looked at your house. If you looked rich they charged you lots of tax. If you looked poor, they said you must have been hiding your money instead of spending it and still charged you a lot of tax. He was in for a disappointment if he thought all our money was in the bank. We didn't have any money, as Mum kept telling me.

He carried the bag over to me and put it on the floor. 'Kneel down,' he said. I hesitated, not sure what he meant. 'Kneel down,' he said again, sharply this time. 'Come on, you've got to do exactly what you're told, remember?'

I knelt down next to the bag. He took the string that

was hanging from my wrist and tied it firmly round the handle of the bag so that my hand was held level with it.

'Right,' he said. 'You hold that handle and I'll hold this handle. It'll look as if we're carrying a heavy bag between us, see?' His voice sounded as if he was pleased with himself, pleased at his cleverness. I held the handle next to me and we both stood up. He held the bag and the bag held me. It was very light, surprisingly light, as if it didn't have much in, but it looked full. He put his other hand on the door catch.

'Remember what I said. We walk down the street, nice and easy. Anyone you know, smile but say nothing. I'll talk if talking's necessary.'

He hesitated, almost as if he was nervous. I had another sudden thought. He probably was nervous. He was in danger, like me, but his was the danger of being caught, being put in prison.

'Right,' he said, 'let's go.' He opened the door and we went out awkwardly, sideways with the bag between us. 'Shut the door behind you,' he said. I pulled it shut. The catch clicked. The street outside had become dark and the street lights had come on so that there were pools of gloom between them. I looked for his get-away car or van but the only ones parked were the usual ones belonging to people in the road. We turned left and walked along. I wanted to ask him where we were going but I didn't dare. It was worse, not knowing, just walking away from home, walking into the darkness.

There was a figure coming towards us, a woman carrying a shopping bag. As we drew closer I saw it was Mrs Gillen. She lived two doors away with her husband. Her children were grown up. My mum didn't like her very much, said she didn't approve of single mothers. 'It's hardly my fault if your father goes off, is it?' she always said. I didn't think it'd be much use shouting for help. What could she do, even if she did believe me? I sort of smiled as we passed. She nodded in her disapproving way. Perhaps she thought the man was my dad. Wrapped up like he was, and on a dark winter evening, he could have been anyone.

'Good,' said the man once we were past. 'Keep going like this and there'll be no trouble.'

We turned left again at the end of the road and crossed the next road. There was no one about. One car drove past but it was a between time: everyone had come home from school but people hadn't started coming back from work. It wasn't the sort of evening to be out in. It was the sort of evening to be by a fire, safely indoors. We turned down the road that leads to the canal. Our feet made hardly any sound on the pavement. It was like walking in a nightmare. I felt a terrible worry, a dead suffocating worry wrapped around me as if I was being buried alive and couldn't escape. We were silently walking through the quiet and dark of late afternoon towards . . . Just silently walking.

'Where are we going?' I asked, not able to keep quiet any longer.

'Not far,' he said. 'Don't worry, you're doing great. Nearly there.'

We came to the bridge where the road crossed the canal. I glanced down. I spent a lot of time here but now the water lay black under the bridge.

'Down here,' he said. We went down the steps from the road to the tow-path. 'Just along here,' he said. Along where? There was nothing along the tow-path this way for ages, nothing but a hedge and a bit of waste ground and then the railway line. It was great for building dens in the summer, or would be, if I was allowed. It would make a good hiding place now, if you didn't mind the cold and the damp and the dark. I did mind. Suppose he tied me to one of the trees and left me?

We hadn't gone far along when we came to a boat. There were lots the other way, proper canal boats, permanent homes for people all year, but on this part of the canal you just got holiday makers spending a night. I thought it was a bit late in the year for a canal holiday.

He stopped by the boat. 'Here we are,' he said. 'We managed that all right. A cup of tea next, I think. Mind the gangway, it's a bit awkward.'

We shuffled sideways up the plank that bridged the gap between the bank and the side of the boat. He jumped down and held my arm to help me. We were standing on the little open space at the back where you steer. It was dark and very quiet.

'Welcome aboard,' he said.

3
The weekend before, mainly
Hannah

I suppose I'd known for a day or two something was up. He had something else to occupy his mind. For months now I'd been the only thing. He was determined to prove he could be the perfect parent once Mum had gone. I knew it would be just another of his crazes and that in time he would take up something else and I'd be tidied away into the roof with all the other embarrassing leftovers. Toad, Mum used to call him. I can remember when she meant it lovingly. It started when he had this sudden thing about reading me my bedtime story. For years it had been Mum's and my special time but then suddenly, he was going to read to me. His favourite when he was a child, *The Wind in the Willows.* He was good with the voices, I'll give him that. Mum came in one evening and started laughing. 'I know why you like that book so much,' she said. 'You're another Toad: boats, caravans, cars . . .'

The time came when she spat 'Toad' out at him as a swear word.

Then she went.

And I became his newest enthusiasm. Ironed blouses for school, all that. I didn't want it. I wanted to be neglected a little, given space to sulk. When Mum left she said to me, 'Are you coming with me, or staying with him?' I stared at her. I knew things were bad but I didn't know she was off. I stared at her. I didn't want her to go. I tried to stop her. 'My friends are here, my school . . .'

'That's your decision,' she said. Then she went.

It wasn't what I meant at all. I ran down the drive

after her as soon as I realized she meant it, screaming after her: 'Mum! Mum!' But it was too late. I stood at the gate not knowing where she had gone, not wanting to go back into the house where I knew she wasn't.

Then Dad started the Perfect Parent thing and I was suffocated. It was worse when the Perfect Parent started parading what looked dreadfully as if it was going to be the Perfect Stepmother. Two of them at me. Two fanatics.

Then, click, he was into something else and I didn't know what. Usually you can't help knowing, he showers you with magazines, swamps you with enthusiasm. This time, nothing. I thought at first it might be work. I knew that wasn't going well, hadn't been for some time, but it was too secret to be that. I needed to find out.

4
Tuesday, about 5 p.m.
Martin

I stood amazed, feeling the wooden floor beneath me shifting slightly. I had longed all my life to go on a boat. We had always lived two streets away from the canal and had always walked along the tow-path. Sometimes we walked into the town centre and passed the boats that people lived in all the time and sometimes we walked into the country and watched the boats moving along with cheerful people on holiday who often shouted out greetings. I always longed for someone to invite me to step on board and travel with them. I think Dad would have liked a canal holiday too but Mum always said sharply that she couldn't see the pleasure in it: housework in a cramped box on a dirty bit of water, that's what she said. Once she'd made up her mind, that was it. No canal holiday.

Now I was, for the first time, actually on board and I wished I wasn't.

The man took some keys out of his pocket and unlocked the door in front of us. 'You'll have to sit in the dark for a bit,' he said. 'Just until we get clear of the town. Mind your head now.' He pushed me gently through the door. There was a step down on to a carpeted floor and two cushioned benches along the sides under windows with a table in one corner. 'Sit down,' he said. 'I'll cut that bag off and you'll be more comfortable.' He took a knife out of his pocket and cut through the string around my wrist. 'There are some things of yours in the bag,' he said, 'and there's a toilet through the first door. I'm going to lock you in and move along the canal until we're out of the town then I'll tie up for the night and get us a meal.'

He went out and I heard the lock click behind him. There were other noises and then the engine coughed into life and the boat vibrated under my feet. It lurched and then I saw a shape pass the window and realized that he was untying the ropes that held us to the bank. The boat lurched again as he got back on and then the engine note changed and we were moving. It wasn't yet completely dark outside and I could see darker shapes passing and occasional lights. I had walked along the tow-path so often, all my life, that I knew exactly where we were. We were going so slowly. You can always walk faster than a canal boat but he was going particularly slowly, the dark, I guessed.

I should have been terrified. I was locked in a boat with a strange man, at night. No one knew where I was. I had no idea what was going to happen to me. I wasn't terrified. I didn't seem to feel anything now. I knew I had been scared witless but now I was calm. It was as if I was doped. It helped that I always did exactly what I was told and had always been told exactly what to do. I sat wedged in the corner and watched through the window as the darkness of the outside world passed slowly, so slowly, and the boat hummed through my body. I saw the full moon rise through the skeleton arms of the trees alongside the railway line, and once the windows of a train strobing past.

I think I must have gone to sleep because the next thing I knew was that the noise and vibration of the engine had stopped and there was a stillness and quietness that helped make everything quite unreal. Then there was a hammering from outside, then another one, then the familiar lurch of someone getting on the boat. The door opened, the light was switched on and the man came in. 'You OK?' he asked. He sat down opposite me, still wearing his cap and scarf. 'Best if you don't see too much of my face,' he said. 'Safest for both of us. A bit of supper now. There are a few of your things in that bag you carried. Have a look while I cook us something. Go outside if you like, but don't try and get off the boat. Just treat this like a short holiday. I'm sure you always wanted to go on a canal cruise.'

His voice was quite friendly. He didn't seem to be dangerous. He went through a door at the other end of the cabin I was in and I heard him making the noises that go with getting a meal. The bag was next to me on the bench. I unzipped it and stared. Then I pulled things out, more and more surprised. My pyjamas. Clean pants and socks and a T-shirt and sweatshirt. Two books. My toothbrush. I stared in horror. These everyday belongings lay on the cushions next to me, somehow more threatening than the man himself. It was as if I had been ripped out of real life bringing ragged ends with me, like tearing off an arm leaves ragged ends. My little scattering of belongings made me feel I would never fit neatly back into my old life again. Then in my despair I thought that my old life had gone with Dad anyway, that I hadn't been complete since then, that I had been more and more of a machine, a puppet.

I got up and looked out of the window opposite, expecting to see the tow-path. There was water glinting in the moonlight. I looked out of the window behind where I had been sitting and saw grass. He had tied up on the opposite bank, away from any possible passers-by. I opened the door and went out on to the little deck area. I didn't recognize where we were at all. We were out of the town and into the countryside. The boat was tied up by a field. I couldn't see anything or hear anything. If I jumped off on to the bank, and didn't fall in the canal, I would have to run across the field. I didn't know where the gate was or where to go if I found it. The man would feel the boat lurch as I jumped and would be after me. I had no chance and he must know it. It was all planned out, down to the toothbrush.

'Supper's ready,' he called out.

He had cooked beefburgers and oven chips and frozen peas. Everyone thinks people of my age never eat anything else. I really don't like them much and I didn't feel hungry. He had taken his coat off but kept the cap and scarf hiding most of his face. He didn't eat with me; he said he'd had his in the kitchen. I hated sitting there with this greasy food lying on the plate in front of me, with him standing there over me.

'Why have you kidnapped me? We haven't got any money.'

'Didn't your dad tell you about his lottery win, then?'

'What lottery win?' I asked. 'He hasn't won the jackpot, has he?'

'No, luckily,' the man said. 'If he had, he'd have so many advisers around we wouldn't stand a chance. No, just a nice little four hundred thousand pounds. I'm surprised he hasn't told you.'

'I haven't seen him this week,' I said, feeling somehow I had to stick up for him, feeling he ought to have told me. We had a phone, didn't we? Why hadn't he told me?

'I expect he was going to surprise you with some wonderful present,' the man said.

I stared at him, suddenly realizing. 'That's why you've kidnapped me. To make him give you all that money.'

'Not all, just half. That's fair, isn't it?'

I didn't see how fair came into it. 'Fair' was that Dad kept his money. Mum would say it was fair that he gave *her* half. It wasn't fair that some kidnapper took half.

'It's no good asking Mum for the money,' I said. 'They're separated, getting divorced. He doesn't live with us.'

'He'll give the money for you though, won't he? We'll ring him up in a moment. When you've finished your supper. I'll tell you what to say.'

This could be my chance, I thought. There must be a phone box somewhere near. If I pretended to be doing what I was told and looked carefully where we went then later I could escape and get to the phone and ring 999 or find a house and hammer on the door, or just find somewhere to hide for a while.

I thought about Dad. It's not easy, looking at your own parents, but I had decided he was like a shaggy old dog that lies in front of the fire. He always seemed cheerful, never looked very smart, let Mum boss him around. He was easygoing, and fun, and I could usually get round him. Then one day, he just wasn't there. He had some little flat on the other side of the town and I used to see him at weekends. When I asked Mum why he wasn't living with us she said I had to ask him. When I asked him, he just said, 'The worm turned at last,' and wouldn't say any more. I didn't like it.

I realized gradually, unwillingly, that I'd known things were bad between them but I'd never let myself see it. They'd had rows, lots, more and more and then almost solid rows until Dad went but they were the kind of rows I could kid myself weren't happening. I suppose it was the kind of people they were. They didn't have shouting and screaming and throwing things rows. The one about the tree-house under the stairs was typical. Mum went on and on, very cold, very sneering, making Dad look silly and small. He sort of shrunk into himself and didn't answer back. Later he'd try to be friendly and pleasant and Mum would just ignore him, as if he wasn't there. If he did exactly what she wanted, it would be OK, but that time he didn't take the bolt off and it was a long time before she forgave him. Later, when I let myself think about it, I knew that she had been coldly going on almost non-stop before he left.

When they were both at home, in the old days before things got too bad, it had been all right. Mum had kept things ticking over and he'd kept things cheerful. Home was comfortable. Now she was too sharp and he was too soft. I hated it. Perhaps with all this money he'd come back. I had to help him keep it.

'Right,' the man said. He had an irritating habit of starting to speak by saying 'right'. I was beginning to get really fed up. I wanted to get everything sorted out. He went on, 'Your father will know you've been kidnapped because your mum will have told him. I've written down what you're to say here, on this piece of paper. If you try to say anything else I'll stop you. And that will just delay everything and I'm sure you just want to get home. You do what you're told and you'll be there quicker.'

He put a sheet of paper on the table. I stared at it. The paper was ragged along one edge, as if it had been torn out of a notebook. I thought stupidly that this might be terribly important. 'Read it out to me,' he said.

> 'Hello, Dad, it's Martin speaking. Don't say anything, just listen. I'm all right and I haven't been hurt. If you do what I say I will be released immediately. Do not tell the police. You will find full instructions in a carrier-bag under your dustbin. Please do what they say so that I can go home. Goodbye.'

'That's fine,' the man said. 'Let's hope he's as sensible as you.' He looked at his watch. I stood up, ready to go. 'Sit down,' he said.

'I thought we were going to phone?'

The man said, 'We are.' He reached into his pocket and took out a mobile phone. He pulled out the aerial and put it on the table in front of me. 'Know your dad's number?'

I nodded.

'Pick it up then and dial. And remember, just say what's on the paper.'

I picked the phone up. My dreams of running across empty fields in the moonlight were shattered. This was a well-planned operation and I had no chance of escape. I pressed the buttons. Dad answered immediately.

'Martin? Is that you? Are you all right?'

The man tapped the sheet of paper.

'Hello, Dad, it's Martin speaking,' I said. I could hear him asking questions but I just went on reading out what was on the paper: 'Don't say anything, just listen. I'm all right and I haven't been hurt. If you do what I say I will be released immediately. Do not tell the police. You will find full instructions in a carrier-bag under your dustbin. Please do what they say so that I can go home. Goodbye.'

As soon as I had finished reading the man took the phone out of my hands, put it up to his ear and listened for a moment. I could hear Dad's voice squawking away. I longed to grab the phone and beg him to come and rescue me but I couldn't do anything. The man switched the phone off and put it down.

'There's nothing more for you to do tonight,' the man said. 'I'll show you where you're sleeping. You could be home this time tomorrow if your dad gets a move on. Bring your stuff with you.'

I picked up the bag with my things in. He led the way through the inner door. There was a neat little kitchen and then another door into a very narrow passage. 'Bathroom,' he said, pointing at the first door. He opened the next door, snapped the light on, and waved me in. 'Your room,' he said. I went in. It was very small: a bunk bed with two drawers under it, a stool, a shelf.

He pointed at the door. 'There's a key if you want to lock yourself in. The doors at each end will be locked so you can't get off the boat and the windows don't open enough for you to climb out. I'd get some sleep; you've had a busy day. Do you want anything?'

He spoke quite kindly. All I wanted was to go home but there didn't seem much point in saying that.

'I'll see you in the morning, then. Don't forget to clean your teeth. Good night!' He went out, shutting the door. I put my bag down on the floor. The curtains were open and I could see myself reflected in the window. I drew them shut. The room was so small I felt claustrophobic, as if I couldn't breathe. I opened the curtains again and put the light off. The moon had moved higher in the sky. As my eyes gradually grew used to the darkness the field outside crept out of shapelessness. I could see a hedge all round it and even a gap in one corner where the gate must be. At least I now knew where to run, if I could escape.

I tried the window. It had a simple screw catch and opened easily, but only enough to get a head out. There was no way my whole body would squeeze through. I gave up thoughts of escape and went to clean my teeth.

I lay on my bunk, trying to get to sleep. I had tried reading but the light was too dim and the book too dull. With the curtains shut I felt as though I was suffocating in a box. With the curtains open the full moon shone straight in. I turned my back on it and shut my eyes. I did what I always did when I was upset: imagined a scene when I was happy. It was something I had learnt in the tense days while my parents were getting ready to split up, when I knew something was wrong, badly wrong, but couldn't face it. I called it Space Travel to myself. I travelled in my mind far away from the kitchen at home, from the waves of anger and bitter reproaches that smashed me down and dragged me drowning under. I travelled to a sunny beach where Dad and I had dug an enormous castle with outlying walls and were desperately defending it now against the incoming tide and Mum was swimming where the waves were just toppling their white crests. She called out to us to come out and join her, it was so good, and Dad called back,

'We'll defend our castle to the last inch!' and we all laughed and laughed . . .

I must have gone to sleep because when I looked at my watch it was nearly half-past eleven. I felt wide awake and very worried. I lay there thinking over the day. If-onlys filled my mind. If only I'd not gone to the shops with the others on Monday, but if you have to go straight home from school every day how do you have any friends? Mum always managed to make it clear without saying anything that she didn't want her tidy house filled with kids . . . If only Mum hadn't come back early and found out, then I might have been late home today and the man would have given up. If only I'd been sure something was wrong when I first came in and gone for help. If only I'd . . . I sat up, wondering. How had the man got in? I couldn't remember any broken windows. Had I been in every room? The front door was locked when I got home; I remembered unlocking it. The back door was shut. I tried to picture it, to see in my mind if the bolts were across, but I couldn't remember.

I shivered in the cold December night. I wanted to go to the toilet. If only he'd brought my nice warm towelling dressing gown from behind my bedroom door as well as my pyjamas. That was what he was doing upstairs while I was tied up, collecting things for me. That was spooky. And how did he know what to bring and where it was?

Suddenly I felt the lurch of the boat that meant someone was getting on or off. I looked cautiously out of the side of the window. I saw the man, well wrapped up again, walking towards me along the side of the boat. I lay down quickly and closed my eyes. Through the open window I could now hear his feet moving through the grass, rustling it as he came closer. The noise stopped. The boat moved very gently. I knew what he was doing. I could see it as clearly as if I had my eyes open and it was broad day. He had leant forward, put one hand on the boat to steady himself, and was looking in my window. I lay still and tried to breathe steadily.

After a long moment the same gentle movement came again and I heard the faint rustling in the grass start up and then fade away. I sat up slowly and looked out of the window. The man was standing about five metres away with his back to the boat, just standing.

I was much too awake now to think of going back to sleep. Wild ideas swept through my mind. He must have left the door unlocked. I could get off the boat and hide in the grass until he moved. I could slip into the canal and swim silently to the other bank. I could cut through the mooring ropes and push off. I knew I would do none of these. I sat up and stared at him through the window.

He seemed to be waiting for someone because I could see him being impatient. He peered at his watch, flashing a small torch at it. He walked up and down, stamped his feet.

At last he saw whoever it was and raised his arm to wave. Then he switched his torch on and waved it around. I could see a shape, a person, walking across the field quickly towards him.

5
Tuesday, just before midnight
Martin

I watched out of the window as the figure approached across the field. The full moon shone overhead, lighting the scene up so that it looked like one of those old black-and-white films they have on TV sometimes. There was something familiar about the person approaching, something that made me leave the shelter of the cabin and creep through the boat until I came to the door at the back. As I had guessed, it was open, letting the cold night air in. I was glad I hadn't changed into my pyjamas: they would have been cold, and they would have shown up in the moonlight. My dark school sweatshirt merged into the gloomy hulk that was the boat.

I leant out, steadying myself by grasping plants on the edge of the bank, pulling at their rough stalks. I rested my chin on the ground, hoping I couldn't be seen. I shivered in the chill.

The figures were close now. In that crisp air sound travelled clearly: the steady rustle of footsteps growing louder. The man stood quite still, waiting. The other walked steadily nearer, nearer. I don't know exactly when I knew for certain, but it was before she spoke.

'Everything go all right?' Mum asked from some distance away.

The man put his finger to his lips and pointed towards my cabin with the other hand. They didn't say anything more until they were close, very close—too close. I shut my eyes and shuddered. I couldn't face what was in front of me. I wanted to bury myself in the ground. I felt like letting myself drop into the slimy water of the canal. The only thing stopping me was the fear of being rescued by my mother and her . . . her boyfriend.

I could shut out the visible world, could shut my eyes, but the sounds travelled sharply towards me, cutting in. Voices screamed inside my head—your own mother has betrayed you! Your own mother!—but the quiet murmurs from outside still overwhelmed them and crept unnoticed into my mind.

I slipped down into the well of the boat and half stooped, half crawled through the door and back into my cabin. I locked the door and lay on the bunk and just stared up at the roof just above my head.

After a while, I don't know how long, I felt the lurch of the boat as the man got back on. I sat up and through the window I watched as my mother walked away, back through the ghostly grey field, becoming smaller as she travelled away from me. I felt so bleak, so alone, worse at that moment than I had since it all began. Mum had always told me exactly what to do, and I had done it, more or less. I had always taken it for granted that what she told was good for me. Then the man had been telling me what to do, and I had known it must be bad for me. Now, what was I supposed to think? Must I still do what I was told?

I went on staring out of the window long after she had blurred into the surrounding darkness. I made myself put the facts into simple sentences.

My father had won on the lottery and not told me.

My mother had arranged for me to be kidnapped to get some of my father's winnings.

My mother had a boyfriend I knew nothing about.

I did not know which of these three facts caused me most pain. Together, they had destroyed my world.

Look on the bright side, Dad had always told me. There didn't seem to be any bright side. I lay down and pulled the blankets over me. Look on the bright side. There must be a bright side, mustn't there?

I slept until the morning. I could see brightness through the open curtains. The sky was clear and the sun was rising. The field shone silver with dew and I knew what the bright side was. I was in no danger. If Mum had arranged the kidnap, I would not be hurt. I would be all right, safe, home at last.

Home. It wouldn't be home. Would Mum tell me what she had done? Would the man suddenly appear as my stepfather? Would they carry on pretending? If they did, would I pretend I didn't know? Could I?

But I was safe.

I lay on my bunk and thought. What would I do now? Would I tell the man what I knew? It might be better not to, yet. And whose side was I on? Did I want Mum and this man, whoever he was, to take Dad's money off him? Was it fair they should use me to do it? Suppose Dad found out I knew? Whose side was I on?

Thoughts went round and round in my head. I'd always tried not to take sides. As well as always saying, Look on the bright side! Dad used to say, There are two sides to any dispute. It used to make me cross when I was smaller. I'd come home from school in an absolute fury at what someone had done to me, demanding that Dad go round and beat a teacher to a pulp and he'd just say, 'Let's talk it through a moment. There are always two sides to a problem. Why do you think she did that to you?' Always so reasonable, Dad. Always slipping out of your grasp, like trying to pick up a jelly. But sweet like a jelly, too.

Mum was different. You knew where you were with her. She took a side and stuck to it. Reason didn't come into it. I knew she was always on the teacher's side, always. It was always my fault, had to be.

When I asked Mum why Dad wasn't living with us she said, 'It's not right that I should speak badly of your own father, but I can promise you there was no fault on my side.' When I asked Dad, he said, 'Well, it's a bit complicated, love. You see, people see things differently. There are two sides to any problem.'

So, whose side was I on?

There was only one answer. My side.

What was best for me, surrounded by people not telling the truth, the whole truth, and nothing but the truth, was to keep my mouth shut.

'Breakfast in ten minutes, Martin,' came the man's voice. 'Bathroom's free.'

That decided me. Speaking to me as if I was at home! Speaking to me as if he had moved in—as perhaps he planned to once they'd got their hands on the money, my dad's money. It was suddenly simple. He'd be less likely to move in if they didn't get the money. My priority was therefore to stop them getting the money. I'd have more chance of doing something to stop them if they didn't know I knew about them. So, act dumb.

I went next door to the bathroom and had a good wash. It freshened me up. I went back and put on the clean clothes he'd brought me. Enough for just one day, so I ought to be going home this evening. Mum was fussy about clean clothes and I was sure now that she had packed the bag before she went to work. And given him a key to get in.

But then what was all that tying me up and banging around upstairs? Why not just grab me and leave as quickly as possible? Perhaps he was just trying to make it look real, making sure I believed it was real. But if it was a real kidnap for the lottery money he wouldn't bother searching the house. Suppose someone came back. Then I realized. He knew no one would come back and he needed to wait for darkness. The banging around was to keep me convinced until it was safe to leave the house, keep me thinking it was real. Well, I knew now it wasn't real, or at least I hadn't really been kidnapped. How could I tell Dad that?

'Breakfast,' the man shouted. Who was he? I began to

think of him as if he had capital letters, The Man. I didn't want to think of him as a person.

I went to the back of the boat. He'd got his silly flat cap and scarf disguise on again. On the table was my favourite cereal and a bottle of the semi-skimmed milk we always have at home.

'I hope that's all right for your breakfast,' The Man said, all innocent.

'It's OK,' I said, all innocent, too.

'I'll put some toast on in a minute,' he said. 'Would Marmite be all right? I'm afraid it's all I've got.' He was laying it on a bit. Would I have been suspicious if I hadn't known though? I nearly said I didn't like Marmite, just to see how he reacted but decided I'd better play it straight.

'Marmite's fine,' I said, without enthusiasm.

He fussed about a bit, brought a cup of tea with my usual amount of sugar, without asking me first, a couple of slices of toast. He ate his in the kitchen again so that he wouldn't have to show his face. I suddenly felt very cheerful. Now that I knew what was going on it all seemed pretty stupid.

I needed to escape and then to get in touch with Dad. Get in touch with Dad. I didn't even need to escape, if only I could get my hands on his mobile phone. But he wouldn't be that careless, would he? He'd expect me to ring 999 if I got the chance.

The Man came back in and sat down. 'Here's the plan,' he said. 'We're moving on a bit, don't want to excite suspicion, especially moored on the wrong side of the canal, so we'll move up slowly as if we're on holiday. I expect you've always wanted to have a canal boat holiday,' he went on. He was so pleased with himself, I realized. He thought he was being so clever with all these little jokes that he thought I didn't understand.

'Not like this,' I said.

'I'm sorry it has to be like this,' he said. 'Perhaps

there'll be another time. Tell you what, once we're on the move, you can come outside. There's no one much around this time of year, and we'll be miles from anywhere. Your father should have the money by noon, and with luck you'll be home by tea. And a day off school, too.'

He stood up. 'I'll get us going. Perhaps you'd clear these things up, wash up for me. And get your bag packed. I want to leave the boat as I found it. Don't want the owner getting suspicious, do I?'

Had he 'borrowed' the boat? My guess was, it was his. He seemed to know it too well. I guessed he was just being ultra cautious.

He went out and locked the door. That was another thing. He had the keys. Breaking in was one thing, but how could he have the keys if it wasn't his boat? I put my dirty things together noisily and went into the little kitchen. I ran a bowlful of water and then had a look around, hoping to spot his phone. It wasn't anywhere obvious.

The boat did its lurch as he got off. I saw his legs pass the window and then the sound of the mooring rope landing on the front. His legs came back. The lurch again and then the motor started, coughed easily into life as if obeying a familiar master. The bank started to slide away. I washed the dishes one by one and dried them and put them into the cupboard. That gave me the excuse to open everything, all the drawers and cupboards in the kitchen. It was all very neat and well equipped.

The back door opened while I was still looking and his voice came through. 'We're just coming to the lock. Once we're through you can come out. You'll need your coat on though; it's chilly this morning.' The door shut. I now knew two things. I knew exactly where we were: coming up to Batlow Lock. I knew he'd be busy for some time. He couldn't slip in quietly and catch me rummaging while we were going through the lock. Where to look to take advantage of this?

This was only a small boat, not one of those proper big narrow boats you get on the canal. It only had the rooms I'd been in already: living room, kitchen, bathroom, bedroom. He must have slept on one of the benches in the living room. He probably had his phone in his coat pocket, but it would be worth a quick look round. I might find something useful.

The engine note changed and we slowed down. Through the window I saw the bank come closer and then felt a slight bump and a lurch and saw The Man wrapping the mooring rope round a post.

I knew this lock well. It had been the turning-round point on our longer family walks, when we had been a family. If we were lucky, and we usually were in summer, we could sit on the bank and watch boats go through. They always seemed so carefree, the people on the boats. I sat between Mum and Dad and envied them the freedom of the open canal. Sometimes I'd push on the great wooden arm of the lock gate. I always hoped the boats would offer me a ride: 'Jump aboard!' one of the holiday makers would shout and I would stand proudly on the boat while Mum and Dad walked back along the tow-path. No one ever offered me a ride. After about quarter of an hour Mum would say, 'Time to be getting home,' and we'd walk back. It was always Mum who decided, I suddenly realized. You have to walk in single file along the tow-path or else you're into the grass and the dog muck and so we didn't talk much on our walks, Mum always in front. Boats passed us, laughing and chattering, and we walked in our single silent line.

I knew we had to go into the lock when it was empty and then rise up to the higher level. When boats were in the empty lock, all you could see were their roofs gradually rising as the water surged around them. I knew there would be a time when The Man couldn't see me at all. There wouldn't surely be anything in the bedroom or bathroom because those were places I could search at leisure. I'd had a good nose through the kitchen. If there was anything to find, it must be in the living room, or whatever you call it on a boat. I went in there and knelt on the bench and looked out of the window.

I could just see up to the edge of the lock. The Man was pushing on the arm, opening the gate. The lock must have been left empty. The boat moved gently inside the lock as he towed it in. While I was waiting I looked round the cabin, planning my search step by step. There wasn't much to search without ripping up the floorboards. It had the table and two benches at right angles to each other. The benches were really padded seats on top of cupboards. That was all. If there was anything, it had to be in the cupboards.

It went dark inside the cabin. Just outside the window the side of the lock shone slimy green. I got up and started searching. The cupboards didn't have any doors; I suppose if they did you'd have to crawl under the table to get in. I had to take the cushions off and then lift up a lid. All the time the boat was rocking quite violently as water spilled into the lock, filling it up. I could see us rising, slowly but definitely rising. I started to panic. I wanted to search everywhere but there wasn't time. The first cupboard had bedding in: pillows, blankets. I slammed the lid and put the cushions back. Light was beginning to come in, brightening the cabin. I pushed the cushions on the second seat, lifted the lid: assorted junk like everyone has somewhere. I could see boots, tools—and then daylight really flooded in and I slammed the lid and tried to look innocent out of the window. The less suspicious I seemed the better my chances later.

The boat rose to the level of the tow-path and

gradually stopped rocking. I could see The Man pushing open the top lock gate. I had had my chance, and found nothing. I went back to the kitchen and finished washing up.

6
Tuesday
Hannah

Dad wasn't in when I got home from school on Tuesday. I hadn't been back long when his lady friend rang and said he'd had to go off on business unexpectedly, he'd tried to phone, there was food in the freezer, would I like her to come over and keep me company? That was a laugh. 'No thanks,' I said. I told her I'd go round to my friend Jenny. She knew I often went there at the weekend when she came and she believed me. I put the phone down. I had no intention of going anywhere. So much for the perfect parent bit.

At least it gave me a chance to have a good rummage through his things but I didn't find anything useful. He has this precious notebook in which he scribbles everything down but he carries it on him: everything in the right place, that's him. Put on the right act. I think that's why there's only one of me. Married people are meant to have babies, people keep hinting. So, he'd have a baby because that's what you do. But I must have been a nasty shock: messy, noisy, untidy, smelly. I'm surprised he coped at all. He certainly couldn't have managed two of us. I'm sure Mum wanted more. She was always broody over other people's babies. I expect that's why Dad likes Carol. I'm surprised she had any, hers must have been a mistake, she's much too self-centred to waste time on anyone else.

After school I went home and got another phone call: still busy, back soon, was I all right? I lay in bed that night and I thought, why doesn't *he* phone me? He's got a mobile, and even if that's gone wrong there are phones everywhere. He's up to something. Then I knew. He'd gone off on his boat, with her. He wouldn't lie to me, but I bet she would. I'll check tomorrow, I thought before I fell asleep, if he's not back.

7
Wednesday, 10 a.m.
Martin

The morning passed slowly. We moved up the canal at less than walking pace. We passed through two more locks and I was shut in the cabin while we went through. We were now well out of the part of the canal I knew. I had a vague idea of where the canal went but if I did escape and wanted to run for help I wouldn't know where to go. We seemed to be in the middle of fields and hedges and didn't even see a road, though sometimes I could hear traffic. The Man had planned well.

He seemed quite chatty and kept pointing things out, mainly birds, which he seemed to know a lot about. He had a pair of binoculars round his neck and kept offering them to me. I always refused. It was a bright morning, though still cold and no one would have thought his being so wrapped up round his face particularly surprising. No one, except there was no one to see him, except me. It was so unreal: the boat moving slowly through empty fields as if everyone else had disappeared from the earth.

I made some tea after an hour or so and I sat in the cabin and went on with my book. I would have liked to explore along the tow-path but I didn't want to ask him, and he would almost certainly have said no anyway. I could feel him wanting to be friendly but I was too cross still at being tricked. I had hardly felt frightened at the time. It was only later, in the days after it was all over, that I became frightened, so frightened. Now, sitting in the cabin, I just became really angry.

We passed under a bridge, the first I think since we had left the edge of the town last night. The Man switched the engine off and we slid silently towards the bank. He tied the boat up at the back and then called to me to come out on to the tow-path. He was standing looking back through his binoculars. I looked around. We were in the middle of nowhere. The canal was slightly higher than the fields on either side and stretched off fairly straight in both directions. There was a thin, leafless hedge next to the tow-path. A road crossed the bridge and there were church spires away in the distance in both directions. The railway line was still there, but further away now.

'This is the danger point,' he said, 'the drop.'

'What do you mean?' I asked, curious even though I was in such a mood. And I felt I had to know as much as possible so that I could grab any chance. I was more and more determined to ruin their neat little plot one way or another. He started explaining, sounding pleased to be asked. Perhaps he was just pleased to be able to show off how clever he was.

'The danger time in a kidnapping is the actual handing over of the money. That's when the police know exactly where you're going to be and can watch the spot carefully. Now, I've told your father to get the money out of the bank and to drive to a phone box that's about a mile away in a small village. We're going to ring that phone box at exactly 12.30.'

No wonder Mum likes him, I thought. They can spend all their time comparing watches.

'Now, this is the clever bit. If he has gone to the police, and people often do, they'll know the area but not the place. This is the place and the beauty of it is, no one can sneak up on us without us seeing them. Your father has to cycle up from that direction . . .'

'I thought he had to drive here,' I said, surprised at catching The Man out.

'There's a bicycle leaning on the phone box, well locked up. The key was in the bag under his dustbin.'

The Man sounded extra pleased with himself. He was enjoying telling me how clever he'd been working it all out. I wished Dad couldn't ride a bike, but he could. We'd had this dream of riding the length of the canal. It was when Mum finally said there was no way we were having a holiday on a canal boat. I was very upset and Dad took me out for a walk along the tow-path. I was very sulky at first because it seemed like making it worse, walking along, seeing the boats, but then he told me this plan he had. We'd cycle from pub to pub, taking about a week to do the whole length and then get the train back. He'd made the mistake of telling Mum. She'd gone berserk, or what for her was berserk—deep-frozen was more like it, accused him of trying to get me on his side. I hadn't realized then that there were sides.

'When we see a cyclist coming,' The Man went on, 'we can check through the binoculars to make sure it's not a policeman pretending to be your father. And we can see in all directions if there's anyone with him. That's why he's got to cycle: you can hide people in cars. If anything looks suspicious we go full speed. They'd need a motor bike to catch us.'

'So Dad will come here,' I said. 'Can I go back with him?'

'He won't be sure we're here,' The Man said. 'We'll be hidden in the boat. He will have the money in a Sainsbury's carrier-bag tied on to a rope and he'll lower it over the bridge on to the tow-path and then cycle back to his car. When he's out of sight, we pick up the bag. If it's all there, you wait on the bridge and I ring him up to tell him where you are once I'm out of sight.'

I think he expected a round of applause or something but I didn't say anything. I had an awful feeling that it was a very good plan indeed.

'You'd better practise looking through these,' The Man said, handing me his binoculars. 'I'll need you to check it really is your father coming.' He pointed over the canal. The road stretched empty between its bare hedges until it merged into the rising land in the distance. He made me fiddle with the adjustment of the binoculars until the distant road leapt up.

'Something's coming,' I said, startled at the sudden movement. He took the binoculars from me. Without them I could see nothing in the distance. They must have been very powerful.

'It's a car, travelling rather slowly,' he said. 'Into the boat. Now!'

He pushed at me quite roughly and I stumbled on to the boat, banging my leg on the side as I went. He pushed me again, into the cabin, and stood quite still in the doorway, binoculars up to his eyes. I sat on the seat, rubbing my leg. I looked out of the window but at first I could see nothing.

He backed in, crouching through the low doorway, still looking. 'Lie on the seat!' he said, sharply. I lay down and watched him. He pushed the door shut and stood against it for a moment, his head turned a little as if he was listening. Then I could hear the car's engine approaching, level with us, and passing. Through the opposite window I caught a glimpse of a small red car driving away. It didn't seem to have slowed down at all.

The Man opened the door and looked out, a quick look first and then a slow sweep round with the binoculars. 'I think it's safe to come out now,' he said. 'Just normal traffic. I hope there won't be much; I can't take the strain.'

We stayed on the boat. There were several more alarms as cars and lorries passed over the bridge but we now had our routine worked out and they didn't seem to unnerve him as that first one had. Perhaps no traffic at all would have been more suspicious, as it might have meant that the police had cordoned off the whole area. A goods train lumbered past in one direction and a passenger one sped towards the town a little later but they didn't worry him. He kept looking at his watch and scanning the countryside with his binoculars. I went to the loo several times, and then made us another cup of tea, and then went to the loo again.

At last time crept round towards 12.30. He looked at his watch more frequently. He took a notebook out of his pocket and tore a sheet of paper from it. He read it through. Then he passed it over to me. 'Your next performance,' he said. 'Same as before. Just stick to the words on the sheet and you'll be all right. And particularly, don't think of trying to say anything clever about where we are—for your own sake.'

I wasn't sure now how serious his threats were. I didn't think he'd hurt me, but I couldn't be sure. I'd read in the papers often enough about stepfathers battering children, and he wasn't even my stepfather, yet. And if he was cornered he might well get desperate. I looked at the sheet of paper.

> 'Dad. This is Martin. Listen and do NOT say anything. If you say anything I have to switch the phone off. You must ride the bicycle that is leaning on the phone box along the road to Milton. After about 1 mile there is a bridge over the canal. Stop there. Lower the carrier-bag with the money in over the bridge on the left-hand side of the road and leave it on the side of the tow-path. Then cycle straight back to the phone box and wait for your next call. If you do everything right I will be released by the time you get there. I will read these instructions again.'

The Man looked at his watch one more time and then took his mobile phone out of his pocket. I stared at it. Of course it was in his pocket. I must have been mad to think he'd put it in a cupboard or leave it lying about. 'You can't trace a mobile call like you can one with wires,' he said. 'It's much safer for all of us. You especially.' He took his notebook out again, checked on the middle page, and tapped in numbers. He waited for the ringing tone to start and then passed the phone to me.

The ringing sound had stopped by the time I got the phone to my ear and I could hear Dad's voice, saying, 'Yes? Hello?' I took a deep breath and started speaking:

'Dad. This is Martin. Listen and do NOT say anything. If you say anything I have to switch the phone off. You must ride the bicycle that is leaning on the phone box along the road to Milton. After about 1 . . .' I faltered to a stop because I could hear Dad's voice going on and on. He was saying the same thing, over and over and eventually it got through to me.

'Martin, there isn't any money. I haven't won any money. There isn't any money.'

I stood looking at the phone, dumbly. The Man grabbed it from me and held it cautiously to his ears, as if it might bite him. Then he slowly and deliberately switched the phone off. I could almost see Dad standing in the phone box, going on and on saying the same words over and over: there isn't any money. What would he do? If he'd listened to my message he'd have had a clue as to where I was, but he wouldn't listen. He'd always been good at listening before, too good. He listened so sympathetically that I used to think something would actually happen. It was years before I realized that he thought listening was enough. And now, when listening might have saved me, he wouldn't listen.

'In the cabin,' The Man said, and pushed me. He locked the door behind me and stepped up on to the bank. I could see him through the window, scanning quickly round the countryside. Then I could see him talking into his phone, his mouth snapping at it. I couldn't hear what he was saying and I daren't open the window. The window that was open, in my cabin, was on the other side. I just watched him snapping and pacing up and down and darting his head round to try to watch the whole surrounding countryside at once.

Suddenly he did a crouching run towards the bridge. I stood up to slide the window a crack open at the bottom while he was out of sight. As I was easing the catch I glimpsed a car, an old green Rover, like my dad's. It could be him! The car was gone, out of sight before I could think. I sank back on to the seat.

The Man came back. He had stopped talking. He untied the boat and jumped on and started the engine. We moved forward, faster than before. I was left locked up inside the boat for about an hour. Soon after we started I heard his phone ring and then him talking but though I leant my ear against the door I couldn't make out what he was saying. I guessed Mum had rung to check up and would now be telling him off for making a mess of it. I almost felt sorry for him.

I tried to notice useful things out of the window. I had an idea that I might be able to escape and so I'd need to know where to run to. I gave up after a bit. I kept switching from side to side, afraid of missing some perfect place. Then I'd see something—a road crossing the canal, a pub and a row of cottages—that would be perfect. I could see myself panting down the tow-path, bursting into the bar, the landlord raising an eyebrow and asking how old I was—and then we'd be past and soon so far away it wasn't worth remembering and I'd start again. After a while I gave up and just worried.

What did Dad mean? Had he really said he hadn't won? He'd certainly said there wasn't any money. Did that mean he hadn't been given it yet? Or he couldn't get so much out of the bank? How much? How did The Man know he'd won? How did he know how much he'd won? Had he told Mum? Had he spent all the money already? Perhaps he hadn't won much? Why hadn't he told me?

I'd seen Dad on Saturday, as usual. Mum liked to get rid of me on Saturdays so she could have a bit of time to herself. I used to get the bus to his flat after breakfast. At first he'd come to collect me but he's not very good at being punctual and Mum got so wound up she said it spoilt her day. It certainly spoilt mine because she'd go for him as soon as he arrived and then he'd get sulky and it took hours before he got cheerful again and we could enjoy ourselves. So now I bus there and we start cheerful. He's usually still in bed when I arrive and I make him a cup of tea. He hadn't said anything about the lottery then.

But if he had won that evening how had they got so well organized by today? And if he'd won the week before, why hadn't he told me? He'd given me some pocket money as usual, but it was the usual amount, and with the usual grumble about how poor he was. I didn't even know if he bought lottery tickets.

The Man unlocked the door. 'I think we could do with a cup of tea,' he said. 'Make us one, will you?' I was glad to have something to do. I made the tea and took it out to him. He'd slowed down now and we were going the same gentle pace as before. 'There's not much to eat,' he said. 'I wasn't reckoning on us still being aboard by now. You could have some more cereal.'

'I'm not hungry,' I said. 'Can't I just get off now? I won't tell anyone. There's not much I can tell.'

'Not yet!' he said. 'I'm not giving up yet. He'll produce the money in the end, and then you'll be able to go.'

'He said he hadn't won.'

The Man laughed. 'He would say that, wouldn't he? A bit selfish, your father, is he? A bit mean? Like to keep it all to himself? None for you or your mother?'

'He's not selfish,' I said.

'We'll see,' The Man said.

We went on in silence after that. I was annoyed at

what he said about Dad because he's not like that. He's a bit unreliable, a bit too easy going, but he's certainly not mean. Mum always accused him of spoiling me but I don't think I'm spoilt. I felt more and more that, if he'd won lots of money, he wouldn't be able to keep quiet about it, that he'd have bought me something I really wanted, like a decent computer.

The Man had a map out now and kept looking at it. We passed under a road bridge and he cut the engine and drifted into the bank. This time he tied the boat up properly, front and back. He'd folded the map up and put it back in his coat pocket or I'd have looked at it, though it probably wouldn't have done me any good. We could be almost anywhere.

We were at a much busier road. Cars and lorries passed almost continuously and we seemed to be on the outskirts of a town. There were buildings quite close. I could see a woman and a dog walking towards us. The Man must have seen her too because he said, 'Into the cabin! Now!'

'Afternoon!' I heard him say, all bright and cheerful as her legs reached the window. 'A bit cold though.' I couldn't hear what she said; she muttered something back at him. The dog stared at me and then she tugged its lead. I knew how it felt.

He came into the cabin. His bright cheerfulness had gone. 'Listen now,' he said. 'This is the dangerous time for you. My plans have gone wrong and I've got to think of something else. It would all have been so quick and safe but your father just had to mess it all up. I'm not giving up; I've just got to work something else out. Now, we need food so I'm going to have to leave you for a bit while I do some shopping. I'll lock you in the bedroom and I'll take your shoes and socks and trousers so I suggest you just stay in bed. Like I said before, you do what you're told and you won't get hurt. I just want to get you back to your mother as soon as I can. You co-operate and it won't be long. Now, how about the toilet first?'

So I was in bed, half dressed. I read my book. There didn't seem to be anything else I could do. Time passed. I guessed it was just a matter of letting time pass. There didn't really seem to be any chance of me getting away. I certainly didn't fancy going out in just a sweatshirt and pants.

Time continued to pass. The Man came back. I got my clothes back. He cooked us a meal, a very late lunch but I didn't feel hungry. We ate it in our separate rooms. He sat looking at his map and scribbling in his little notebook. I read, and dozed. Time passed. It did, but so slowly you could notice each separate second as it went by.

I thought about time passing, its erratic speed, the way you can't call it back, the hymn we sang at school once: 'time's ever-rolling stream'. Streams are two-way things. We could travel back along the canal now if The Man wanted, and we would arrive where we started, but there was no way we could travel back to the moment when we started. You can travel both ways in space but not in time, unfortunately. 'Time's never-moving canal' didn't sound quite as good. Time passed, as it wanted.

8
Wednesday, about 5 p.m.
Martin

Time had passed, until the day was over and it was dark. I don't remember ever sitting and watching the light before, the way it thickens gently, as if at the end of the day it all comes home and settles down; the way objects at a distance fade away; the slowness of it. After a while The Man drew the curtains across and I couldn't watch it any more.

At last time seemed to have passed enough for The Man to let something happen. He had been looking at his watch a lot again and finally it told him what he wanted. 'I'm just going out a minute,' he said. 'I won't be long and I'll be in sight, so don't think of doing anything stupid.'

He went out and locked the door behind him. As soon as he had gone I went to the bed-cabin and switched the light on in there. I went back into the main cabin and switched its light off. I hoped he'd think I'd gone to lie down. I went over to the tow-path window and moved the curtain. I couldn't see The Man at all so I risked sliding the window open, slowly, gently. I realized suddenly that this window opened wider than the one where I had slept last night. It looked wide enough for me to slide out.

I edged my face out until I could see along the tow-path. The Man was in sight, as he had said, but he had his back to me. What should I do? Could I get out? Could I get out in time, unseen? Where would I go? He was between me and the way up to the road that the street lights lit up. The other way the tow-path stretched away until it rounded a corner. That way was quite dark. Somehow I didn't fancy the idea of a furious Man chasing me into the blackness.

Before I could make up my mind he started forward and I could see a figure coming down the path towards him. Mum. I nearly shouted out but I remembered she was on his side, part of his plot. I kept quite still, hoping my head would be invisible against the bulk of the boat. I could hear their voices, but not what they said. They seemed less lovey-dovey tonight. She seemed more her normal self, sharp, cold. It wasn't long before Mum raised her voice. She's never exactly been a shouter, but her voice penetrates, goes straight through you, straight through brick walls. Dad shuts up and goes what she calls sulky but she becomes more and more audible, and all without yelling. You can hear her streets away when she really gets going. None of the teachers at school are in the same league; I used to wonder why she bothered with the telephone. Now I could hear quite a lot of what she said, especially when she started walking towards the boat. It was like overhearing a phone call at first, just one side of the conversation:

'. . . no money . . . believe that . . . who told you . . .' and there'd be words I couldn't hear because her voice dropped a bit. It was obvious what was happening. The Man was telling her that Dad said there wasn't any money. She just didn't seem to believe him, Dad I mean. She never had a high opinion of Dad's truthfulness. I didn't realize that when I was young, of course, but looking back I remembered too many times when he'd told her something and she just looked at him and raised her eyebrows, or times when she'd asked me an innocent-seeming question that sort of double-checked what he'd told her. Later, in the time of the great rows she'd called him a liar to his face. So it wasn't difficult to believe that she thought he was just lying.

'. . . hardly cut his ear off and post it to him, can we?' she said, all too clearly.

The Man mumbled something.

'Don't keep saying "put pressure on him"! How can we put pressure on him?' A pause while The Man said something. Then another clear laying-down of the law, but below full volume. They'd come a bit closer to the boat by this stage. 'You're not to frighten him any more. You've done enough.' Another pause. I could almost hear what he was saying now. 'It's going on too long,' she said. 'Get it finished this evening, one way or another. Martin needs to come home.' Thanks, I thought. You might have realized that before starting this whole thing. And then she spoilt it by saying, 'The longer it goes on the more dangerous it is for everyone.'

I drew my head very cautiously back into the cabin and it was lucky I did—or so I thought at the time. Now I wonder what would have happened if I'd called out to her then, burst into tears or something dramatic. At the time, though, I still had this idea that I could beat them at their own game.

'He must not know I'm involved,' she said, quite close to the boat.

'He's no idea at all,' The Man said. 'Why should he suspect?'

'I suppose you'd better try it,' Mum said, 'but if it doesn't work, that's it. You'll have to think of one of your superior plans to get Martin home without his father going to the police.'

'I'll work something out,' he said, and they walked away towards the bridge and their voices faded. Mum seemed to have calmed down because I couldn't hear what she was saying any more. I slid the window back down but didn't fasten it up. I thought a quick get-out might be useful. I went and lay on the bed and pretended to be reading.

A little later The Man got back on the boat and called me into the main cabin. 'Sit down, Martin,' he said, speaking in what was meant to be a pleasant way. I sat down and he sat next to me, but at the other end of the seat. Ever since we'd left my house he'd always been careful not to crowd me, not to seem threatening.

'I've got this problem,' he said. 'Well, we've got this problem.' We? Is he going to tell me about Mum, I wondered suddenly? Have they changed their plans? 'You and I have this problem. We both want to get you home to your mother as soon as we can, don't we?' He was speaking to me now as if I was some little child.

'Yeah, I'd like to go home. 'Course I would.'

'That's right, of course you do. Now the problem is money. It's cost me quite a bit to set this up, and I was a bit short already. Now, I need your father to produce the cash. He's being very silly, pretending he hasn't won. I know very well he has. I'm not being unreasonable; I'm not asking for all of it. I just want a share.'

'Well?' I asked.

'What I ought to do is cut a bit of you off and send it to him, show him I'm serious. A finger, an ear. That's what kidnappers usually do. The thing is, I don't want to have to do that. Seems a bit unfair on you.'

'Thanks,' I said. I was glad I'd heard Mum going on at him. I thought my ears were pretty safe.

'But, if we could convince him I would do it, that might be enough,' he said.

'We?'

'What I'm suggesting is a bit of play-acting. We've agreed I've got to convince your father that I'm serious, haven't we? Right, there are two ways I can do it. One is really to be serious, but that way you get hurt. The other is to pretend. That way you don't get hurt, your father pays over the modest sum I'm asking for out of his winnings, and you go home to Mummy. So, will you help me pretend?'

I sat in silence for a bit. Partly I was acting: acting

confused and uncertain. Partly I was wondering if I could do this to Dad. If it worked he'd be frightened for me. He must be frightened for me now, I realized suddenly. Mum knew it was all a game, but he didn't.

I knew what I had to do, but I didn't know if I had the courage.

'What would we do?' I said.

'I'll write you a suitable speech and we'll ring him up and you can tell him what danger you're in. The more convincing you are, the quicker it'll all be over.'

'I suppose so,' I said.

'I'm sure that's the right decision,' he said. 'Now let me write something down for you.'

While he was writing I went over and over in my head what I could say to make Dad realize what was going on. If I wasn't careful The Man would stop me as soon as I stopped reading out what he'd written and then I'd be worse off than before. I don't think I trusted him that far, even if Mum did.

The Man tore the page out of his notebook and pushed it over to me. 'Read it!' he said. I picked it up and stared at it. It looked weird, like something a maniac might write. It was some time before I realized he'd put in sort of stage directions in capitals:

> Dad this is Martin SHOUT help me help me CRY Dad he's got a knife QUIET TERROR he says he'll cut my ear off SHOUT Dad give him the money CRY please please

'What do you think?' The Man asked. He sounded pleased with himself. 'Think it will work?'

I stared at the piece of paper. He was expecting me to do this to my own father? To do my best to terrify him? If Dad believed it he'd go out of his mind. It wasn't the sort of message I could quietly slip in hints about the canal and about Mum and about it being a con trick. Did Mum know what this man was doing?

'What's he supposed to do?' I asked. 'It doesn't say how to give you the money. Is it the same as before?'

'I'll ring him about five minutes later,' he said, 'and give him full instructions. I'll disguise my voice, put on an accent. That way, he won't know what I've done to you, keeps up the pressure. We'll use the same idea, but a different bridge, make him leave the car and walk. That way no one can be too close to him.'

I stared at the piece of paper. There was no way I could do this. Perhaps I didn't have to. Mum had said it had to be over tonight and that if his next plan didn't work, that was it. I had to find a way of stopping this.

Then he gave me the way, so easy, so obvious I couldn't quite believe it.

'I've got to make a phone call first, set things up,' he said, 'and then we'll get on with it. No point hanging around waiting.'

He stood up. 'I'll just go on to the tow-path to be out of earshot. The less you know the better. And it'll give you a chance to practise your lines without feeling embarrassed. I want a good performance.' He rested one hand on the piece of paper and leant forward. 'You've been all right so far, remember. Not been too bad, has it? Right, let's not make this unpleasant.' He turned in the doorway. 'I won't be long. Let's make it good.'

He went out and locked the door behind him and I felt the familiar lurch as he stepped off the boat.

I made myself count to twenty, slowly, and then I edged the window up and looked out. He had walked a little way along the tow-path away from the bridge where he had talked to Mum.

I had to get out of the boat. I had to get out of the window. I thought it was big enough, but it would be a squeeze. A slow squeeze. The Man could rush back and grab me. Push me down into the black water of the canal. Let the boat ease itself over me as I fought to keep the water out. I couldn't do it. He would hold the boat against the bank while I struggled to find my way under it in the mud and weed and blackness. Struggled desperately to find the other side.

The other side! The boat had two sides, two windows. I slid this one shut and crossed the cabin to the other side. The catch was stiff and I had a moment of panic but then it suddenly moved, grazing my finger. I opened the window and looked out. There was a narrow ledge running round the boat just below me, and just above the water. I had to get my feet on that, and I had to do it now.

I turned round and came out feet first, feeling for the ledge. I clung on to the frame of the window and edged my body and then my head out. I kept myself bent down below the top of the boat in case The Man was looking this way. There was a hand rail running around the top of the boat and I slid my hands along it, edging my feet after them. It wasn't far to the little deck at the back of the boat. All I had to do now was to get off without being seen.

I peered round. The Man was still on the tow-path. He was taking little paces up and down, talking into his phone. I couldn't stop to think, to plan. As soon as he turned away I jumped on to the bank and ran along the grass verge to the bridge, to its safe blackness where I could disappear from sight and have time to think.

There was a darker shape in the darkness under the bridge. Someone. I nearly turned and ran back to the boat, had half turned when my mind caught up with my eyes and I realized what I saw. There was someone, about my age, on a bike, legs on the ground to keep it up. A watcher in the shadows.

I stopped, not sure still which way to go: up on to the road, past the girl along the tow-path, back to The Man? Then the watcher spoke. A girl's voice, a very quiet girl's voice.

'What were you doing on my dad's boat?'

I stared.

She put her hand out and pulled me into the greater darkness under the bridge. I stared at her. In the silence I could hear The Man's voice as he spoke into his phone. 'Who are you?' she said softly.

'I've got to get away,' I said.

She got off her bike and turned it round. 'This way.' We came out on the other side of the bridge. There was a gateway in the hedge that ran along the tow-path. She pushed the bike through and laid it on the grass. I stood and watched, not sure what to do. I could see the shape of The Man's boat through the arch of the bridge but I couldn't see him. I would be able to see him, his moving darkness, when he got back on the boat.

'I'm Hannah,' she said, almost breathing into my ear. 'Who are you? What's going on?'

I just stood there. I didn't know what to do. Was she helping him? Was she there as a guard? Would she tell him where I was? The path to the road was on his side of the bridge. If I tried to run down the tow-path one of them would cycle after me and catch me easily. Could I run faster than them over the field? And what would be on the other side of it?

A car went over the bridge; its headlights dazzled me for a moment. 'You're Martin!' Hannah said. 'You are Martin, aren't you? You look just like your mother. Is she on the boat? Is that what's going on?'

'How do you know my mother?' I asked, stupidly. I knew what the answer was so I don't know why I said it.

'Because she's carrying on with my dad, that's why I know her. And they're up to something, I know they are. That's why I came all this way. I saw he'd moved the boat and I guessed he'd come this way. I was going to catch him at it.'

I wasn't sure in the darkness, but I thought she was crying. She couldn't be part of the plot, even if she did know more of what was going on than I did. Everyone knew more than I did.

'I think he's talking to her on his phone,' I said.

'What are you doing here? What's going on? Why are you running away?'

I saw The Man, Hannah's father, silhouetted in the archway. I pulled her back to the hedge. 'What's going on?' she demanded.

'They've kidnapped me to get money off my dad. They say he's won the lottery.'

'I knew they were up to something. That makes sense. He's desperate for money. Where's Carol?' Carol is my mum, Mrs Carol Ashling, shc's meant to be.

'I'm not supposed to know she's involved.'

'Typical devious pig,' she said.

I heard a shout from the boat. I pulled Hannah through the gateway and we tried to blend with the hedge. It was prickly and the long grass soaked my trainers.

The Man came running under the bridge. He stopped and must have been looking around. We stood quite still. 'Martin?' he called. 'Come on, Martin. I'll get you home safely.' We went on standing still. Hannah was obviously not going to betray me. The Man turned and ran back under the bridge. Moments later I saw him crossing the bridge, running. 'Martin!' he was calling.

'On the bike,' Hannah said suddenly. 'Ride to the next bridge and wait for me there. Go on! It won't matter if he catches me.'

She pulled the bike up and pushed it through the gateway. I couldn't see The Man. I pointed it away from the boat and started peddling like mad. That was a mistake. The tow-path was uneven, rough, and the bike hit a pothole and slid from under me, throwing me off. Fortunately I went into the hedge and not into the canal or the splash would have brought him running. Hannah was there, picking the bike up.

'You OK? For God's sake be careful. Take it easy!'

I set off again, slowly.

I had only gone a few metres when Hannah came running after me. 'Stop!' she whispered. I braked. 'The back light,' she said. 'It shows so clearly. Switch the dynamo off.' She seemed to have stopped crying, seemed almost excited.

'I won't be able to see anything. It's not safe.'

'You can put it back on when you're round a corner.'

'I'd rather run,' I said. 'You have the bike. We might as well go together.' I didn't like the idea of going into the dark by myself with no way of escape. The canal was on the left, the hedge on the right, The Man behind, and anything could be in front.

'If you go in front there's no need to run,' she said. 'If Dad comes after you I can delay him while you get away. I'll tell him I was worried when he wasn't at home and came to look for him. And it's the truth.'

I turned and walked on. Even that wasn't very easy. It should have been; there was only one path. The blackness seemed to be an obstacle I had to push through. After a while we came to a long bend on the canal and I had to be careful to keep on the path. It was so uneven that it wasn't always obvious where it ended and the verge began.

'Stop a minute,' Hannah said. 'It should be safe to put the lights on now. I'll go in front and cycle slowly. You follow but keep listening behind.'

I let her pass me and then had the red light to follow which was easier but I kept turning round, thinking I could hear footsteps behind me and then had to hurry to catch up.

It seemed a long time before I saw the black shape of the next bridge. Hannah stopped the bike and waited for me. We stood side by side and stared back the way we had come. Everything was silent.

'You'd better tell me what's going on,' she said.

We stood under the bridge and I started to tell Hannah what I knew. I said I'd been caught by a man waiting inside my house when I came home from school. I suddenly realized as I was speaking why I hadn't seen any signs of breaking in to warn me: there weren't any. He hadn't needed to break in. Mum had given him a key. I had really known this before but it sank in now for the first time that my mother had coldly planned it all in advance. That upset me a lot and I couldn't go on for a bit. It really brought it home. I was surprised she hadn't cut my ears off herself.

'And he brought you to his boat?' Hannah prompted.

'Yes. We came up the canal and stopped for the night. Then I saw my mum come across the fields and talk to him, to your father. They seemed very friendly.'

'They are that all right,' she said. 'Didn't you know?'

'He made me ring my dad up to tell him where to bring the money. He said he'd won on the lottery but when I rang up Dad said he hadn't and that he hadn't got any money. I was supposed to ring and scream and try to convince Dad that I was going to be harmed, make him bring the money. That's when I escaped, and then met you.'

'And they don't know you know Carol's involved?'

'No, I'm sure they don't.'

'I think we'll go home,' she said.

I stared at her. Was she in the plot as well? 'But why?'

'Where else? I don't think it would be a good idea for you to go to your home. That's probably the first place they'd look for you. I expect Carol will be sitting there waiting for you to turn up.'

'Why not my dad's place?' I asked. I still wasn't sure I could trust her, that I felt she was on my side.

'Suppose he's not there,' she said. 'And Carol could be sitting outside in her car, waiting there, thinking you'd run to him.'

I thought that was exactly where Mum would be. She always said I preferred him to her, took his side. There was too much of a risk. I couldn't go to either, in case.

'We could look carefully, and wait,' I said.

'I don't fancy hanging about outside people's doors at night waiting for them to come home,' Hannah said. 'We can get into my house. There'll be no one there. It's the last place they'd look for you, even if they thought you knew where it was, and I can easily hide you in my room. Personally, I'd like to be indoors and warm and have a drink. Of course, you don't have to come with me.'

'Thanks,' I said. 'That sounds great.'

9
Wednesday Evening
Hannah

I had plenty of time to think as we went back home. I'd come out that evening after yet another suspicious phone call from Carol. I thought I'd just check up on the boat. When I saw it wasn't there it did give me a bit of a shock. I'd suspected he was having this big thing with her but they'd been very careful in front of me. The boat was obviously where it had all been happening.

I set off up the tow-path without thinking. Dad had always gone that way and I thought I'd find him. And I did. I stood in the shadow of the bridge and just watched and then Martin came crawling out and ran straight into me and I knew then that I could get my revenge. That was all I thought about at first: getting my own back on the pair of them. Martin seemed such a cowed little worm that at that stage I didn't think he'd be any use. I was going to shove him in a cupboard and forget about him while I plotted.

He fell off the bike and snivelled and moaned and I nearly just shoved him in the canal and left him. Then I rode ahead and he stumbled along after me and I could think. I thought about what a mean selfish person Carol seemed. She came in that first time all bright and cheerful and sensitive, just as if she'd read all the books about being a new step-parent but it was all false. She fancied Dad and his kitchen and his smart road.

'I've got a boy your age,' she said. 'I do hope you'll be real friends. We must get them together soon, mustn't we, John?'

Well, they had got us together. I wanted my mum back. I couldn't bear to think about her, about the way

I'd run out too late and she was gone. She'd rung me once when Dad was out. I think she'd tried other times but Dad kept her from me. She'd been crying while she was talking, said things were difficult, said she loved me . . . said she hoped things would work out . . .

I thought, perhaps I can help them to now.

10
Wednesday, about 7.15 p.m.
Martin

It seemed to take hours to get back but when I looked at my watch later and worked it out it can't have taken much more than an hour and a half. By the time we got there I had passed the point of tiredness and was moving on auto-pilot. It was better once we got to the town with the street lights and then the pavements and the last bit seemed easy. Hannah led me to a street not far from mine but the houses were larger, detached, and surrounded by gardens.

'If I say "Run!" then belt for the canal,' she said. 'I'll come and find you there when I can.'

She pushed open a gate and we walked up a gravel drive. The house ahead of us had none of its lights on. Large trees were close to the sides of the house, making it seem shut in and secret. She leant her bike up against the side of the house and went up to the front door. I hung back a bit, ready to run, though my legs were so tired I don't think I could have run far at all. She opened the door and switched the hall light on. 'Dad?' she called. 'Dad?' There was silence inside the house.

'Come in,' she said.

I walked up to the door and looked in. She was already walking into a room at the back. I shut the door behind me, wondering if I had walked into a trap but too tired to care any longer. 'Tea all right?' she called.

'Great,' I said. 'Thanks.'

I followed her into the kitchen and into a different world. It was full of machines and gleaming surfaces and matching colours. Mum would certainly have fallen for the kitchen in a big way, whatever she thought of The Man.

'Have a seat,' Hannah said.

I sat at the table and watched as she made the tea. She was efficient and organized, like her father. I wondered if she looked like him, as she had said I looked like Mum. She was skinny and had dark hair to her shoulders and her face was freckly and friendly. She brought two mugs of tea over and then fetched a pot of sugar and a tin with a cake in, a couple of plates, and a knife.

'Hot sweet tea, best thing for shock,' she said, and put two spoons of sugar in my mug. I sipped it and felt it spread through my tired body, making me relaxed and drowsy.

'You don't go to my school,' I said, almost as a question. They lived quite close to us. I ought to know her.

'I'm afraid I go to the High School,' she said. The High School was a smart private school for girls on the other side of town. No wonder I didn't know her. The High School went with the kitchen and the boat. I sipped my tea, feeling out of my depth in every way.

'I'm sorry about my father,' she said suddenly.

'Why would he want to do it?' I asked. 'You don't seem exactly short of money.'

'He lost his job last month. He's desperate.'

'Where's your mother?' I asked, and immediately wondered if I'd been tactless.

'She walked out, when things started to get difficult. Dad's got a nasty temper.'

She didn't explain and I didn't like to ask. 'My dad left,' I said, 'or was driven out. I live with Mum and see him at weekends.'

'I know,' she said. 'I see a lot of her at weekends.'

'I didn't know,' I said. 'I must be stupid.'

'Parents! Who'd have them?' Hannah said. 'They've been really cruel to you, haven't they? Splitting up,

Carol carrying on with my dad and not telling you, and now kidnapping you to get your dad's money. You must have been terrified.'

'It's funny,' I said, 'but I feel more frightened now. What am I going to do?'

'What are *we* going to do, you mean. We ought to get our own back on them, teach them a lesson. More tea?' I nodded and she took the mugs over to the tea pot and filled them up.

'How?' I asked when she came back. She was getting more cheerful by the minute and now seemcd to be really enjoying herself.

'We know everything and they don't,' she said. 'Just think what they don't know.' She ticked things off on her fingers as she spoke. She wasn't a quiet, restful person at all. She was hardly ever still but was always moving. 'They don't know where you are. They don't know that you know Carol's involved. We must be able to use that. They don't know that you've met me.'

'I don't want to go to the police,' I said.

'Yes, but that's another thing they don't know. I bet they think you're in a police station now pouring out your story. That's what you would have done, if it had been real.'

'So,' I said, thinking it out, 'Mum would have to be at home and your father would have to leave the boat . . .'

'So we could safely use the boat,' she said. 'I know all about it. I ought to, I spent enough time on it.'

'I couldn't walk back there,' I said, 'not tonight. Where would he go? Would he come here?'

'Not safe. Once the police found the boat they'd know who he was. So . . .' She paused, thinking. 'He can't leave the boat; he'll have to move it, as far as possible, find somewhere to hide it or get it off the canal and on to the river. He couldn't leave it and come here. And Carol wouldn't dare come here. This is the safest place there is.'

'What about my dad?' I said. 'Should I phone him and tell him I'm all right. He must be worrying.'

'Let him,' Hannah said. 'He's a parent, isn't he? He left you. He won a fortune and didn't tell you. Let him sweat a bit. If you tell him, then the others are bound to find out. This is too good a chance to waste.'

I wasn't sure she was right. I wasn't sure about anything. Perhaps Dad hadn't won. He'd kept saying there wasn't any money. But how would it all end, anyway? We couldn't really just say sorry and pretend nothing had happened. Did I want Mum to know I knew what she'd done to me? Did I want to go home anyway after what she'd done? Would she go to prison if the police found out? It might all be clearer in the morning after a good sleep.

'Have some cake,' Hannah said and pushed the tin over to me. I picked the knife up at the same moment as the phone rang. She jumped and stared at me. 'I'll have to answer it,' she said. 'I ought to be here.' She picked the phone up and went on staring at me, as if I could help her.

'Hello? Yes, Dad, it's me. I haven't been out. No, I haven't.' I sat watching her, the knife poised in my hand. It seemed heartless to cut a slice of cake when she was obviously being yelled at. He must have rung her earlier and not got an answer. I could see from her face that she was pretty unhappy at what he was saying. I remembered she'd said he had a nasty temper. She held the phone a little away from her ear and I heard his voice ranting on. She didn't seem to be able to say anything. The voice was casting a spell over her. She drooped and I thought she might tell him everything. I waved the knife at her, signalling that she should put the phone down. It seemed to break the spell and she put it to her face again.

'I'm in the kitchen. There's a boy with a knife pointing at me.'

I dropped the knife in surprise. She winked at me, grinning suddenly. 'He says he was on your boat and saw a letter addressed to you and got our address. He says you are to wait on the boat and I am to ring you later with his demands. He says that if you come near the house he'll ring 999. He says I'm to put the phone down now.'

She stopped speaking and slowly put the phone down. 'I hope that was a sensible thing to do,' she said.

'He'll ring Mum,' I said. 'She'll come round. Has she got a key?'

'Yes, she has. I'm sorry. I couldn't take him shouting at me as if I'd done something wrong. What's he think he is?'

'We'd better go,' I said. 'Find somewhere to hide.'

'That's easy,' Hannah said. 'We'll hide here.'

I stared at her. 'Hide here?'

'Yes, don't you see? It's brilliant. We make it look as if we've left but we hide somewhere until she's gone and then we're safe here. Make them sweat a bit. Now, let's have a bit of a struggle.'

She pushed the table sideways and knocked a chair over. She picked up her mug and dropped it on the floor. It shattered and tea spread over the tiles. She took my mug and washed it up. She looked round, considering.

'Door open?' I suggested.

She opened the back door and looked out. I heard the sound of milk bottles falling and rolling. 'That's the kidnapping,' she said. 'Now, what was I doing before? We don't want her looking upstairs too carefully. TV. Bring the cake, and the knife of course.'

She went out of the kitchen and I followed her. She went into the front room and closed the curtains before she switched the light on. She put on the TV and jumped on a sofa in front of it and wriggled around and dropped a cushion on the floor.

'Upstairs,' she said.

There was the sound of a car pulling into the drive, crunching over the gravel. I found I was tip-toeing up the stairs even though the carpet absorbed any sound. Hannah grabbed my arm and steered me across the landing. A little light came up from the hall below but this was a shadowy space surrounded by open doors, each leading into blackness.

'We'll go under my bed,' Hannah breathed into my ear.

'Hannah, are you there?' Mum called out downstairs. It was a very strange feeling. My own mother walking into a house, using her own key, calling out to someone I'd never heard of until that evening. Me, standing in shadows above her. 'Hannah?'

'Come on,' Hannah whispered again, but we were both held by the need to know what was happening downstairs. Somehow I knew Mum had gone into the kitchen, perhaps the slightest tap of her shoes on the tiles, then her voice sounding further away. Then there was the unmistakable clicking of shoes crossing tiles. I tugged at Hannah until at last she moved. We went through the left-hand doorway. The curtains had been closed in here already and I moved from shadows into total darkness. Hannah held my arm tightly and I shuffled a few steps forward. Then she pulled me down to the carpet and I felt the edge of a bed.

'Crawl under,' she whispered.

I moved carefully, feeling in front of me. As I moved light suddenly shone in. I turned my head and realized that the landing light had been switched on. I could now see to move more quickly. We squeezed ourselves up by the wall at the head of the bed and waited.

I could see the brightly lit doorway cut off by the side of the bed. Suddenly without warning because of the thick carpet everywhere, shoes and the bottom part of legs appeared. 'Hannah?' The room light came on but the legs didn't move, didn't move for a long time it seemed as I hunched motionless against the wall. The light went off again and the feet went.

Hannah uncurled herself and slid forward. 'Where are you going?' I asked, suddenly anxious. I didn't want to be left and I didn't want to move.

'We must know what's going on,' she whispered back, and went on crawling. I followed her from the security of the bed into the searchlight beam from the doorway. She got up and stood behind the door and gestured to me to stand next to her. She looked through the crack by the hinges. 'The light's on in Dad's room.'

'There's no sign of her . . . No, and it looks as if there's been some kind of a struggle.'

'The phone by Dad's bed,' Hannah whispered, but I had worked that out by then for myself. It had been a shock hearing Mum speak out loud suddenly. I had thought for a moment that she was talking to us, had seen us. Every word was clear, as always with Mum.

'If it is Martin he's not going to hurt her . . . Frankly, I can hardly believe it. I wouldn't have thought he'd have the guts . . . Of course we can't go to the police . . . I don't know where he will have taken her. He might be going home but I doubt it. He'll probably go to his soft father. He always used to run to him when he was in trouble . . . I'll go round and have a quiet look. You can be sure the one place he won't be is here. Is your car still at Milton? Right. Leave a light on in the boat just in case they go that way . . . They'll think you're still on it if it's lit up . . . Yes, and come and meet me at Robert's flat, that's where they'll be going for sure. I'll ring your mobile if anything crops up. Bye!'

There was silence and then the slam of a door downstairs. Hannah went across to the window and peered round the edge of the curtain. I heard a car starting up. 'She's driving away,' she said. 'Wasn't that brilliant? We've hooked them!' I sat down on the edge of the bed, suddenly totally exhausted again.

'But what do we do now?'

'So many choices,' she said. 'Your house will be free if they're both going to your dad's. The boat will be empty. We could get your bike and we could cycle back to it and move it somewhere else. What do you think?'

'I don't know.'

'In fact,' Hannah said, 'the best thing to do is stay right here. She as good as told us it was the one place they wouldn't look.'

'All right.'

Hannah was pacing around, restless, unable to sit still or be quiet.

'Let's get your bike while we can,' she said. 'That way, we're mobile. Come on!'

We went downstairs and out of the front door, only minutes after we had heard it slam. She closed it quietly behind her. 'Walk on the grass,' she whispered. 'She might have suspected something and sneaked back.'

I wished she hadn't said that. I had been feeling safer, knowing The Man was travelling back from his boat and Mum was driving over to Dad's flat to see if I was going there. Now every bush could be hiding her. She might jump out and grab me at any moment. I walked as quietly as I could, ready to run for it.

At the gate Hannah paused, looked out, and then said in a normal voice, 'It looks all clear. Which way?'

We walked under the street lamps towards my house. There didn't seem to be anyone around although there was still the hum of traffic on the main road. We turned into my road and I hesitated, looking for the car, but Mum's usual space outside the house was empty. The house itself was quite dark. I stopped at the gate, unwilling to go any nearer. Home had become a trap.

'Where's your bike?'

'Down the side passage.'

'I'll get it,' Hannah said. 'You keep watch. Is it locked?'

I took my keys out of my coat pocket, thankful for all Mum's nagging. I held the padlock key out to her and she took it and went into the darkness of the passage. A moment later she was wheeling my bike out.

'We should have brought mine,' she said. 'That was a silly mistake.'

We turned and started walking back the way we had come. Car headlights turned the corner. 'Down!' Hannah shouted, and dropped to the pavement. I crouched awkwardly on my bike. The parked cars hid us from the road. The headlights passed without stopping and we got up and went on walking, back to Hannah's house.

11
Wednesday, about 9.45 p.m.
Martin

Hannah's house looked just the same when we got back. Mum's car wasn't visible. We left my bike just inside the front gate where it would be out of sight to anyone driving in. I was going to lock it but Hannah told me not to in case we needed to make a quick getaway. I stood there next to it while she went to fetch hers. Seeing them both there, ready, made me feel safer.

Hannah was making all the decisions now; I was so tired I could hardly move and I certainly couldn't think. She led the way into the house through the back door. Then Mum . . .

12
Wednesday night
Hannah

I should have expected a trap. I should have realized:
—that Carol had seen us under the bed;
—that she knew Martin too well to believe for a moment that he would have been able to kidnap me, would even have thought of it;
—that the phone call from Dad's bedroom was just too audible and just too clear in its instructions;
—that she left the house and drove away just too obviously.
I should have realized, but I didn't. I can't blame Martin; he was just too bombed out to think at all. It was all my fault.

As we walked into the house there was this great cry of triumph and a great sweeping out of a corner and Martin was grabbed. She tried to grab me as well but I twisted away and stood back. She held Martin tightly, not as you'd want your mother to hold you after a kidnapping but with her hands gripping his upper arms and away from her, and Martin stood tightly, rigid. I'd not seen them together before. They did look alike, had the same face and the same way of holding themselves, but, even in that moment when she caught him, a moment that seemed to stretch on for ever, you could see that they weren't really the same person. She was cold and reserved by nature. Poor Martin was reserved from fear, from years of training. He wanted to collapse into his mother's arms, but daren't.

Then she was shouting. If I was Martin I'd be able to write down every word, pause, gesture, but thankfully I can't. He just stood and took it while she abused him.

The general drift was that he was an ungrateful nuisance, which must have boosted his self-esteem no end. Various themes were developed at some length. There was his father's complete selfishness, coupled to Martin's resemblance to his father. There was Martin's disobedience and his thinking he knew best. And running through and through there was the inconvenience she had been put to. Poor Martin just stood there, taking it stony-faced, not saying anything, even when she shook him and said, 'Well?' This seemed to annoy her, she seemed to expect a reaction of some pathetic kind from him, and I realized that in his own way he had started to stand up for himself. It was a pretty negative way but he hadn't actually collapsed inside. He stood, head down, staring at the floor, silent, numb.

She kept shouting at me to 'Come here!' but I didn't. I didn't run away either. I knew I had got Martin into this trap and I had to get him out, though I had no idea how. I kept far enough out of reach and shouted, 'Let him go! Let him go!' and watched her in case she suddenly made a grab for me, and waited.

What happened was that she pushed Martin upstairs and locked him in the bathroom. As she turned with the key in her hand I knew I'd be next but I still couldn't think what to do for a moment, and then I suddenly did know. She didn't come for me, though. She went into Dad's bedroom and I heard the phone ting as she picked it up. She was going to phone Dad to tell him. I knew what to do about that, too. I pulled the plug out from the extension socket in the hall. I don't think she realized what I had done because she went on trying to get through. I crept quietly out of the back door while she was busy.

I had worked out what to do. I had a big advantage at the moment: I was on my home ground and knew it better than she did. She had known there was a key in the bathroom door but did she remember that there was also a bolt?

I stood under the bathroom window and looked up at the light. I knew exactly what to do: all the books tell you. I picked up a handful of gravel and threw it up. Some of it rattled on the glass and all of it fell back on me, which wasn't in the books. The window slid up and Martin's head poked out.

'Bolt the door!' I called up.

His head disappeared and I heard Carol calling like a snake beguiling its prey: 'Hannah, is that you? Come here, will you? I need to talk to you about this.'

The other thing the books all tell you is that up a tree is the safest place to hide as no one looks up. I hadn't climbed a tree for a year or two, but I remembered this one well. If I was Martin I'd describe each handhold but all I'll say is I was up and pressed against the trunk before Carol came round the side of the house. She'd found Dad's torch and was shining it around, searching the bushes. I began to wish all this was happening in summer so that the leaves would hide me but I kept quite still and she didn't look up, even at the bathroom window. Martin was looking out, his face almost level with mine but about two metres away. We both watched as the torch beam led Carol round the corner.

'I've bolted the door,' Martin said.

I looked at him, framed in the window. It seemed to be stalemate. He couldn't get out and they couldn't get in—except they surely could batter the door open? We had a little time, but not very much. They didn't know where I was.

'What now?' Martin asked.

'I'll get you a key,' I said.

That was what I had remembered. Seeing Carol turn away from the bathroom door had brought Mum back sharply. Dad had been on his security binge after some burglaries in our road: new locks on the doors, window locks, all that. His enthusiasm got diverted into a new garden shed before he got security lights and burglar alarms fitted but as part of his mania he went on about the bathroom, wanted to fit one of those locks you can open from the outside. 'Suppose someone's taken ill in the bath,' he kept saying. Mum wouldn't have it. She thought they made a house look like a hotel. In the end he gave way for once but got a spare key cut and put it, carefully labelled, in the kitchen drawer. He totally forgot about the old bolt and left it there. That was typical really: incompetent efficiency. You could see that he and Carol were made for each other. Mum was different: incompetent but somehow things got done without any fuss. Usually. In the end. Or else they weren't important any more.

'There's a spare key,' I said. 'I'll fetch it when it's safe and chuck it to you. Then you can let yourself out.'

'But she'll catch me again.'

'I'll cause a diversion,' I said. 'I'll work something out. Just be patient and don't unbolt the door.'

And that's what happened. The great thing about being outside a house at night is that you can see in perfectly—as long as the person inside is too agitated to think of drawing the curtains—but no one inside can see you. It was just too easy to get the key and get up the tree again and even to throw the key in through the window.

As I did, Dad's car drove in through the gate, its headlights filling the garden. I kept still and hoped he wouldn't think of looking in the tree. I didn't fancy being stuck up there on a December night while he waited below. He didn't, of course. He switched his lights off and ran into the house to his darling Carol.

The next bit was easy, too. After they'd come up and found the bathroom door was bolted they banged and shouted for a while and then went downstairs again. I thought it was time to get Martin out in case Dad decided to break the door down. I wasn't sure that he would because he's so touchy about his things. He doesn't really like anyone using anything. I remember when we got our new cooker. He stood over Mum and fussed. 'Don't pull the pans on the hob, lift! Look out, it's going to boil over. Don't leave the oven door open!' Mum smiled and got on. Pans boiled over for her regularly. I couldn't quite see Dad lifting a heavy hammer to his door, splintering the wood, damaging the paint . . .

'Be ready, Martin. I'm going round to the other side of the house and I'm going to break some windows. I'll scream like mad. As soon as you hear me, unlock the door and get to the front gate. I'll wait by the bikes.'

It all went so well. I pulled a couple of stones out of the rockery. I screamed like mad and flung them at the windows, which broke with a satisfying racket. Dad and Carol came racing round, the neighbours opened their window and leant out shouting, 'What's going on? Are you all right?' and I waited at the gate, holding the bikes. Waited, and waited.

I climbed the tree again. Martin was shaky. Panic was getting to him. Dad had left the key in the outside of the door and he hadn't been able to open it. I was going to have to come up with a better plan.

I talked it over with Martin. At least, I talked. He wasn't contributing much at this stage. 'Let's approach this logically,' I said. It helped saying it out loud. It calmed him down a bit and stopped me from going round and round in circles in my head. 'We've got three choices,' I said. 'One, we can get you out through the door. Two, we can get you out through the window. Three, we can rescue you after they have let you out of the bathroom. I don't like Plan Three. It's too chancy, especially now there are two of them. Plan One means I have to come into the house and turn the key. Plan Two means a ladder. The ladder is padlocked in the locked garage. It's heavy. It will make a noise. It's impossible. So, Plan One it has to be. I have to come in and get you out.'

I spoke calmly, but I wasn't sure I could do it and if I was caught as well we'd had it, finally had it.

13
Thursday, about 12.15 a.m.
Martin

My life was going round in circles, moving from one lock-up to another. Long, long ago, it seemed, I had locked myself in my 'tree-house' under the stairs to escape The Man. Now I had locked myself into his bathroom to escape my mother. I didn't like to think about the fact that she had also locked me in, to be able to hand me over to him.

And my only hope was his daughter, perched in a tree outside the window.

At least there was no pretence now. It was them against Dad, and me as their weapon.

They had come and shouted at me through the door and banged and threatened. They had gone away. There had been the sound of breaking glass and screaming. I had unbolted the door and found the key in the lock so that the one Hannah had thrown me wouldn't work. I was almost glad. I didn't have to do anything. I didn't have to run through the house and be pounced on.

Then Hannah said she was coming to get me out.

14
Thursday, the early hours
Hannah

I hadn't told Martin my big worry; I thought he was jelly-like enough already. I can't blame him. I was running around smashing windows and shouting, having a great time, while he was shut up, caught, at their mercy. If I had been my dad I'd have locked the doors to keep me out. Luckily, Mister Efficiency wasn't much use in a real crisis. He was amazing at planning in his little notebook but if one thing didn't work out exactly right it seemed to throw him. Mum used to take charge then and tactfully suggest a solution.

At least he still hadn't closed the curtains. At one time he'd had this economy thing and was always saying that we had to make sure we closed the curtains to keep the warm in. He rushed round the house at the first hint of the light fading and pulled them so that they overlapped exactly. There was a great row when he came home one day late from work and my room was the only one with them closed. I didn't like the blackness reflecting me back, knowing I could be seen by any secret watcher, but I never thought about the rooms I wasn't in and Mum just said she hadn't got round to it yet.

The back door was unlocked. I went in cautiously and took the key out and put it in my pocket. I certainly didn't want to be locked in the house with no escape route. The only light now came from the sitting room; Dad's fanaticism about economy had left him still switching lights off automatically whenever he went through a doorway. Voices came from there: Carol and Dad. I walked stealthily across the hall carpet past the half-open door and on to the stairs. I stopped because I heard my name. I hadn't been tuned in before; I'd been concentrating on getting to Martin. Dad had said something about me, something about what about Hannah?

'She doesn't matter,' Carol said. 'What do you think she's going to do? Come bursting in followed by half-a-dozen policemen? She's out there somewhere, sulking. Smashing the windows was a bit of temper. She's like you: blows up and then calms down again. She'll be in before long, all sorry about the glass, you'll see.'

No you won't, I thought.

'Martin's safe in the bathroom,' she went on, calmly, soothingly. 'All we've got to do is persuade Robert to hand over the money.'

'He says he hasn't got any money.'

'But you know that's not true,' Carol said, as if to a silly child. 'You told me. He and his friends in the pub celebrating.'

'That's right,' Dad said. 'They were. Falling about laughing they were; they'd definitely won the lottery. Someone mentioned spending four hundred thousand and they all fell about laughing again.'

'So,' Carol went on, all maddeningly patient, all controlled, so cold, 'we know he's won a lot of money. He knows you've got Martin. He doesn't know about me and he doesn't know about Hannah running around like a demented banshee.'

'How did Martin and Hannah meet up? I thought you hadn't told Martin anything about us yet.'

'I haven't. I don't know how. It doesn't matter at the moment.'

'She knows too much,' Dad said. 'She and Martin have probably pooled their knowledge and they know what's going on. I don't like it.'

'Look, we'll just say this was a practical joke that got a bit out of hand. No one can prove otherwise. I'll fix Martin, don't worry. He'll believe and say just exactly what I tell him. That doesn't matter. What does is the money. You've got to get it out of Robert quickly. If this goes on much longer something really could go wrong.'

And it will, if I have anything to do with it, I thought. Poisonous woman!

And him! No wonder Mum left home! But why hasn't she been back for me? She can't think I'd rather be with him, can she?

Carol was going on, calm, cold: 'John, you need the money. Just remember that. You're in a desperate financial situation. It's not your fault; it's the recession. You've worked hard, goodness knows. You're owed something. Why should that layabout have all that for doing nothing? And I'll tell you one thing for sure, if you don't get the money you can forget about us. I've had enough scrimping and saving. I'll get some out of him one way or another and if I have to ditch you to do it, that's too bad.'

Dad groaned. I went on, up the stairs, thinking hard. I certainly didn't want her moving in. And what about Martin? Was he supposed to move in too? And I just had to take all this? Well, Miss Key the Kidnapper's Daughter ought to be able to fix his little game of Happy Families for him. I had to get to Martin's dad, with Martin if possible. I had to get in touch with Mum and for that I had to get my hands on the little notebook Dad kept in his pocket.

I turned at the top of the stairs and leant over the banisters. The voices were going on but I couldn't make out what they were saying. I tapped quietly on the bathroom door and turned the key. 'Martin, it's me, Hannah,' I whispered.

I heard the bolt slide and the door opened. He stood in the doorway, white-faced, trembling. Great, I thought, a lot of help he'll be. (I know that was unfair but it's what I thought at that moment.) I pulled him out of the bathroom and closed the door and locked it again. Well done, Miss Key, I thought. I took Martin's arm and led him to the top of the stairs. The voices were louder. They were louder because they were out of the sitting room and into the hall and coming towards the stairs.

I pulled Martin back into the darkness of the landing, towards the greater darkness of a doorway. I was suddenly dazzled as the light was switched on and we stumbled into the dim safety of my dad's bedroom.

'Martin!' Dad shouted. 'Listen to me.' Poor Martin could hardly help listening. I gripped his hand in case he broke. 'All I want is for you to make that one phone call. Then your mum will take you home and you can forget the whole thing. She'll explain it all to you. It's a bit complicated, grown-ups' business you know. Don't worry about it; there's really nothing for you to worry about. I'm sorry you've been frightened, bit of a bad joke really. I'm unlocking the door now and I want you to unbolt it and open the door for your mum. She's here. She'll tell you.'

'Open the door, Martin, and stop messing about,' Carol said, and really motherly she sounded too. I gripped Martin tightly to stop him shaking. There was silence for a few moments. 'He's not going to,' Carol said quietly.

'Unbolt the door now or I'm going to break it open,' Dad shouted. He was getting near breaking point. 'Right, I'm going for my tools to break my way in. Your mum will wait at the bottom of the stairs. No one's crowding you. You've got two minutes or things will get much more serious.'

I looked through the crack in the door by the hinges and saw them going downstairs. I picked up the phone. 'What's your dad's number?' He was telling me when I remembered. I had cleverly unplugged this extension downstairs. The phone was dead and we were trapped upstairs. Miss Key had not cracked it yet. They would come upstairs, break into the bathroom, find it empty, realize what had happened, and catch us.

I tugged Martin. There wasn't time to explain. We had to be poised in my bedroom and run down the stairs the moment they went into the bathroom. That would be the only chance we'd have.

The landing was brightly lit. One of Dad's safety things had been the importance of bright lights on stairs. It conflicted with his economy drive, but safety won. Carol was standing half-way down the stairs, her back to us. I could hear clattering coming from the utility room where Dad was collecting tools.

Martin was pulling back but I didn't dare whisper to him. I tugged harder and pointed across the landing towards my bedroom. At last he seemed to understand and followed me.

'Is he out yet?' Dad called.

I could see Carol turning and dropped to the floor, pulling Martin down with me. We were out of her line of sight as long as she didn't move.

'Martin, time's nearly up. Better come out now!'

I felt Martin flinch and grinned at him to keep him going. I didn't dare stand up in case she was looking our way or in case Dad came into the hall. I tugged again and we slid over the soft carpet—thank goodness Dad had had prosperous days!—towards my room.

Once we were safely in I leant Martin against the wall, put my mouth to his ear and whispered. He nodded as I explained. We heard them coming up the stairs. I edged towards the doorway, tensed, gripping Martin. They went past.

'This is your last chance, Martin. Come out now!'

I saw Dad put his shoulder to the door, turn the handle. I heard his cry of surprise as he fell into the room. Carol darted after him. I leapt for the stairs, pulling at Martin. We lost our footing and tumbled down, over and over each other, shoes clattering against the banisters, and rolled on to the hall floor. I jumped up and saw their two faces open-mouthed over me. I grabbed at Martin who was still lying there.

'Martin, come here!'

He hesitated, conditioned to his mother's command, but I pulled and caught him off balance and he came stumbling after me, through the kitchen, out of the back door, round the house. We ran crying down the drive towards our bikes.

15
Thursday morning
Martin

Hannah had been great. I would have been completely stuck without her, completely at their mercy. She got me out before anything awful could happen. It must have been the relief that made me cry, away from the feeling of being completely cornered, with Mum shouting at me and The Man threatening.

We pedalled madly, Hannah leading the way. She kept turning corners, going from one side street to another. I was completely lost, had no idea where I was. It was like going for walks with my gran when I was little. She hadn't liked the canal—stagnant water and too much dog dirt lining the tow-path—and took me round the streets near our house. After a while she'd say, 'Oh dear, we're lost, oh dear!' When I was very small I believed her and was always amazed that we did, always, find our way home. Now I know she was just pretending so that the dull suburban streets would seem more exciting. So many things got worse after she died.

They were exciting enough now. It was like being in a film. Everything was black and white and blurred in the street lights and our speed. There was no one about. Most of the houses were dark and silent. I didn't know where home was at all.

Hannah suddenly braked and I ran into her. 'Car!' she said. 'Quick!'

She got off and pushed her bike into the front garden of the nearest house. I followed. There was one of those tiny lawns, a few bushes, a low brick wall. She dropped her bike on the grass and crouched behind the wall by a bush. I followed.

I could hear the car now and then its headlights shone down the road, creating sharp shadows. I ducked. 'Keep still!' Hannah said. As the car passed I saw Mum at the driving wheel, staring ahead, and then it was gone, the light first, then the noise. We stood up.

'That's one,' she said. 'I wonder where the other is?'

'We can hear the cars coming,' I said.

'That's it! Clever of you, Martin! She's driving round, revving away at the corners, headlights blazing, and he's sneaking about trying to catch us unawares.'

'But we'd hear the car.'

'He'll be on his bike,' she said. 'You remember his bike? Part of the Great Plan to collect the ransom? He'll be sneaking silently around while she distracts us.'

'His bike's at the phone box,' I said.

'Not his best bike. That's in the garage.'

I looked up and down the road. There were circles of light under each well-spaced lamppost and deep pools of darkness between. Anyone could be watching silently from those shadows, poised on a bicycle, waiting to corner us.

'What are we going to do?'

'Hide,' Hannah said. 'We're the only people moving on the streets. We stand out. They'll go on looking all night, especially round your dad's place. We need shelter and then, in the light with people around, we'll be safer.'

'Hide where?'

'We'll take sanctuary. Come on, follow me.'

It wasn't far but at every moment I expected The Man to leap out at me. Every piece of darkness could have hidden him and the lights just created darkness. We didn't see Mum's car again, which somehow made it worse. Two of them were after us, and we didn't know where they were.

Hannah pushed open an iron gate. It shrieked in the silence of the night. We were in a churchyard, gravestones leaning towards us in the gloom, each one a perfect hiding place for a waiting attacker. We pushed our bikes up the path, leant them on the church wall, and went into the porch. The church door was locked, of course.

'Welcome to St Barnabas,' Hannah said.

It didn't feel very welcoming. We sat close to each other to keep warm and dozed a little, at least I did and when I woke Hannah was quiet. I don't think she was asleep because when car headlights shone across the graves and lit up the black arms of the trees stretching towards us I felt her stiffen beside me until they passed.

It was a very long time before it started to get light, a very long time. Even when it was light we knew we had to wait until people were around before it was safe to move. We started talking in the pale grey of dawn. Something about the misty start to a new day, something about having survived so far, about sitting wedged together in the corner of the porch, loosened my tongue and I could say to her what I had never been able to say to anyone else. When well-meaning teachers had asked if anything was worrying me I'd just said, no, I'm fine, there's nothing wrong.

I told Hannah about Dad, about how much I missed him at home, about the way home was cold, efficient, lifeless, about how bored I was at home, how friendless I felt at school because I was never allowed to wander about with mates but had to account for every moment. I cried, but I didn't mind crying. The place and time didn't seem real.

Hannah told me about her mother going, about how she longed to see her, to have her arms around her, how she feared she didn't love her or else why hadn't she been in touch more?

The sun turned the mist pearly and then it shone through. We smiled at each other through our tears. 'That's better,' Hannah said. 'Now, let's plan.' She looked exhausted, but wound up. I realized suddenly that I wasn't the only one who'd had a world-destroying shock. On top of her mother's desertion her father had done this to me—her father. The day was bright but it stretched ahead of us with danger out there, somewhere.

'We've got to get hold of your dad,' she said. 'I've been thinking about it and it's the only thing to do. There's a phone box just round the corner.'

I took some coins out of my jeans' pocket and lined up the ones that the phone would accept. Hannah kept looking up and down the road, nervously. I picked up the receiver and put the first coin in. I dialled Dad's number, heard the clicking and then the phone ringing, ringing.

'He ought to have an answer-phone,' Hannah said. I was going to say he couldn't afford one but then I realized that perhaps he could. The phone rang and rang. I put the phone down and stared out in despair. What was I going to do?

'Let's look round the graveyard,' Hannah said suddenly. 'I like graveyards.' I followed. I didn't like graveyards. I didn't like thinking of all those people rotting quietly under the grass, the worms, the bones patiently lying, waiting . . . There wasn't anything else to do so I followed.

In the daylight it looked different. The gate had a sign on it: no dogs in the churchyard please. The grass was neatly cut; the path swept. Someone cared here. Someone lavished time and thought on the dead. Somehow it made me even more depressed. Hannah went round chanting out all the rhymes she could find on the gravestones as if she was in church. I leant on one near the gate and stared back at the phone box. There must be someone I could ring.

I could hear Hannah's voice from the other side of the church. Perhaps an irate vicar would burst into the graveyard to rebuke the mocker and all our problems would be solved by his miraculous powers. There didn't seem to be anyone around. It was a country of the dead. Perhaps they rose at midnight, shaking earth and mould off their silvery bones, and went about their awful business. Perhaps Hannah wasn't mocking. It might be some church thing you did. I wouldn't know; we never went.

A boy of about my age cycled past, bright orange bag over his shoulder: delivering newspapers in a normal world. We should be on the front page. I didn't want to be on any page of a newspaper for everyone to read.

Her voice grew louder and she came round into sight again. She saw me leaning against my gravestone and came over. I must have looked pretty depressed because she said, 'Cheer up! While there's life there's hope!'

'What are we going to do?'

'Seek divine guidance, of course,' she said. 'Stand up and turn round. Read out your inscription.'

I thought this was just another of her silly games like chanting round the church. I pushed myself off the stone and turned towards the gate. It was no good staying here.

'Yes! That's it!' she said.

I looked round. She was kneeling in front of the stone, tracing out the lettering. Then she read out in a clear, normal voice, quite different from her chanting of the other stones, 'I Have Gone To My Father's House.'

She turned and looked at me. 'Do you have a key to your father's flat?'

'Yes.'

'Does Carol?'

'No.'

'That's what we are meant to do. We go to your father's house, like the stone says. Can't you see? It's the stone you leant on when you needed help and it answered you.'

I thought she was daft. Did she think that this

inscription had been chosen more than a hundred years ago just to give me a message? It was just coincidence. Then I remembered that Dad collected coincidences, had a little notebook in which he wrote them down, had hundreds of them. They fascinated him. It started when I was a baby. I was ill with something and a woman rang up and said, 'Hello, Carol, how's Martin?' and for a moment Mum thought it was Gran but it turned out to be some other woman with a daughter called Carol and a grandson called Martin who wasn't well. Dad couldn't get over this and that's when he started collecting. I used to collect for him too. This is another one for him, I thought.

'It might be the best thing,' she said. 'Think about it. We'd have a safe base, a phone, we'd know if he came back. Where else can we go?'

'OK,' I said, 'but I'll try phoning once more first.'

Hannah patted the gravestone. 'Thanks William Elphin,' she said. We walked back, wheeling our bikes, carefully shutting the shrieking gate behind us, and tried the phone again, but again there was no reply, just the ringing, ringing.

'He's not there,' I said, unnecessarily.

'We'll try in a bit,' she said. 'He may have just popped out. Let's try his office next.'

I rang the exchange and they told me the number. We tried this and a snooty secretary said he wasn't there and she didn't know where he might be.

The streets had come to life now with people going to work: cars, cyclists, pedestrians. It should have felt safer but somehow it didn't. I led the way to Dad's flat, keeping my head down, not wanting to see what was around me.

I stopped before the last corner and Hannah pulled up beside me. 'It's round there,' I said.

'Is there somewhere safe for the bikes?' she asked. I shrugged.

'There are some kept in the side passage. That's where I leave mine if I bring it.'

'Not good for a quick get-away, though. Suppose we leave them here in case we have to make a run for it?'

We got off our bikes and locked them to a lamppost. I straightened up and tried to feel brave and decisive. 'Right, let's have a look,' I said. We walked to the corner and looked round. The road looked normal: cars parked, not much happening. The house Dad's flat was in was about half-way along, a large red-brick building with a dusty privet hedge in front and a small garden that rubbish collected in, blown from the road. No one seemed to care enough to pick it up.

Hannah was flicking her head from side to side, turning round every couple of steps. I thought she was bound to attract attention behaving so suspiciously and tried to disappear into the hedges and fences but anyone curious would have wondered why we weren't in school anyway and perhaps Hannah just looked like a truant.

I went straight in at the gate and up the path. I already had the outside door key in my hand. I took one quick look round, and tried the door. It wasn't locked, as it often wasn't in the daytime. I took one quick breath and opened it. The hallway was empty. Dad's flat was on the ground floor, its front door at the foot of the stairs. I found the right key and opened the door as quietly as I could. 'Dad?' I called, softly. There was no answer. I could feel Hannah breathing just behind me. I took a step into the flat.

There was a narrow dark passage inside the door that ran from the front of the house to the back. It didn't have any windows so Dad usually kept the doors open so that light came from the rooms. There was a sitting room at the front of the house, then a bathroom, then a small kitchen looking out at the back, and a bedroom opposite that was under the stairs. It was usually pretty untidy and not very clean though Dad always went on about being just about to get sorted out. After Mum's mania for order and hygiene I found it a relaxing change.

Hannah stepped in behind me and closed the door. I had an irrational feeling of being trapped but if anyone was here it could surely only be Dad?

'Hello?' I called again, louder. There was no reply. I pushed the door to the sitting room wider and looked in. There was no sign of anyone, no sign of anything unusual, just Dad's usual mess. We looked in all the other rooms but everywhere was the same.

'Well lived in,' Hannah said. I didn't know if she was criticizing the mess or, like me, found it comforting.

'He's not here,' I said, unnecessarily.

'We need a back way out,' Hannah said.

'In the kitchen.'

We walked back and I pointed to the back door. It just had a lock and the key was in it. Hannah turned it, opened the door, and looked out. The back garden was as depressing as the front, but tidier. It was just grass surrounded by a fence. The backs of the houses in the next road rose up on the other side of the fence at the bottom. The only way out really was down the side passage and through the front garden. There was certainly no hiding place and no quiet, quick escape. Hannah sighed rather obviously and shut the door again.

As we went back down the passage I took my coat off and hung it up on one of the hooks opposite the front door, as I always did when I came to see Dad. I noticed that his usual coat wasn't there. The flat was warm so he hadn't turned the heating off, or even down. Hannah took her coat off and hung it up next to mine. We went into the front room and sat down. I think we both felt rather lost. I had hoped that Dad would be at home, that he would sort everything out. Now that he wasn't we were really no better off, except that the flat was warmer and had a phone.

I felt so weary suddenly. I had another of those waves of exhaustion and depression that had started sweeping over me. I felt there was no point in thinking of anything. We were powerless. It was all out of our hands.

'Actually, I'm starving,' Hannah said. She got up and I heard her rummaging around in the kitchen. She came back waving a couple of tins. 'Food in ten minutes. We're not going to starve here at least.' She looked at me, slumped in the arm chair, not responding to her, staring at the floor. 'Go and have a bath,' she said suddenly. 'It always cheers me up. But don't be too long.'

It turned out to be a good idea of hers. I lay in the hot water feeling it relax me. Mum had always insisted on me having a complete change of clothes at Dad's—'Suppose it rains and you get soaking wet'—and I was fresh and calm when Hannah shouted that food was ready. She had set it out on the table in the sitting room: baked beans on toast it was and I was ready for it.

16
Thursday afternoon
Hannah

The day passed. Nothing happened. There were occasional noises from upstairs which made me nervous until Martin explained. There was an elderly woman, a widow, living upstairs. His dad reckoned she tried to mother him. They used to go up to her flat sometimes for old-fashioned afternoon tea. Her flat was bigger as it had most of the space the large downstairs hall took up, which gave her a second bedroom. His dad kept asking her to swap flats with him so that there'd be a room for Martin, but she always pretended he was teasing her and treated it as a joke. Martin said he thought the real reason was she liked being able to see what was going on from her upstairs window, was really pretty nosy.

'Could we go and see her?' I asked.

'Would you explain?' he said, and that was enough answer and we were silent again. It was so dull the tension got to me and I began to wish something would happen.

As I was thinking that the phone suddenly started to ring. It was on the small table next to me and, without thinking, I picked it up. As soon as the ringing stopped I knew I had done the wrong thing but then it was too late. I stared at the phone as if something horrid was about to crawl out of it. What did come out was Carol's voice: 'Robert? Robert, are you there?' I saw Martin looking horrified and making signs at me to put the phone down and I lowered it slowly until it clicked and the voice was gone.

'I'm sorry,' I said. 'I don't know why I did that.'

'At least you didn't speak,' he said. 'It may not

matter. She might think there's something wrong with the phone. We'd better plan out what we're going to do.'

Martin's dad wasn't a believer in net curtains and there was a clear view into the street from the table. This was just as well as it meant that I saw Carol coming before she saw me. She must have parked her car down the road a bit and used Dad's mobile because I suddenly saw her on the pavement coming fast towards the house.

'Down!' I said and pushed my chair back and dropped on to my knees. Martin gave me a startled look and got down too. We squeezed under the table.

The doorbell rang, loud, demanding. I looked at Martin. 'Aren't you going to answer it?' he said, and giggled.

There was a knocking on the window above us, a steady, attention-seeking knocking. If only there'd been gravel in the front we'd have been able to hear her footsteps. Was she still there? Would she look in the back windows? Was there anything to give us away?

The doorbell rang again. Then the flap on the letter box in the inside door rattled. Then her voice came. 'Martin, I can see your coat. I know you're there, Martin. It's no good hiding. Come on, the game's over.'

I sat frozen. How stupid! Thanks to Martin's tidy hanging up of his coat, the result of all Carol's naggings over the years, we had been found yet again.

'Martin, I want to talk to you. Come on, we need to sort things out. Come on, dear, open the door.'

Silence.

'Martin, just open this door now!' she shouted through the letter box.

I put my hand on his arm. 'Let her sweat a bit,' I whispered.

I thought we probably would have to open the door in the end. I couldn't see any other answer. Hostage-takers came out eventually when the police surrounded them.

We had nowhere to go and would crack in time. Our only hope was Martin's dad coming home. Was it better to hold on and hold on, or to give in before we had to? Could we bargain our way out? I didn't think I'd be able to bargain with Carol. So, go early or go late?

'Martin, have you got someone in there with you?' Silence. 'If there's someone else in there could they shout out?' Silence. 'Martin, have you done something silly? I can help you if you have.'

She was pretending again, perhaps just trying to muddle everything up. The reality was simple: she was the enemy and we had to escape from her. It would suit her to confuse us, to confuse Martin especially. She knew that he hadn't 'kidnapped' me. She knew perfectly well who I was, had known me much longer than Martin had, knew more about me than he did, but talked of me as 'someone' as if she didn't know anything. I couldn't believe she was going on pretending, going on treating me as just someone to use for her wars against Martin's dad. She was getting it too complicated. What was she supposed to know anyway? It sounded almost as if she was pretending she didn't even know he had been kidnapped in the first place. She didn't sound concerned for him, as she ought to have been.

'Say nothing,' I whispered.

'Talk to her? Me?' Martin whispered back, showing some spirit at last. 'If we keep quiet she may go away.'

One thing that worried me was whether we would know if she went away. Stuck under the table as we were we might never know if she went quietly out and away. We could move when it got dark but I hardly wanted to sit cramped under the table until then. I needed the toilet for one thing.

'Next time she speaks we'll move from here,' I whispered. 'Somewhere we can see the door. If the flap on the letter box is down we can tip-toe past to the back of the house.'

'We could hang something over the door so that she can't see in.'

'Do you think she's certain we're here?' I asked.

'Yes,' Martin said. 'The phone, my coat. It makes sense. Where else would I be?'

'Come on, Martin,' Carol started again. 'Whatever it is you've done, we can sort it out. Trust me . . .' and so on she talked, trying to break him down. As she talked we came out from under the table. We went out into the passage and sidled along the wall. I knew we had to do this but I had a fear of Carol actually seeing him, of him seeing her. I felt that if their eyes met he would be in her power, would have to do as she said, as he had all his life so far. Rebellion isn't easy.

'That's enough, Martin. Open the door at once, do you hear me?'

Triumph was rising in me. All the times I'd been spoken to like that, all the temper, all the tellings-off I had endured, all the ways adults had put me down, the way Mum had just gone into almost-silence, all this kept my mouth shut. Carol couldn't bear not to be answered; I knew that already. To keep silent was our greatest weapon against her. I stood shaking while she went on.

Suddenly she stopped. Then I heard her speaking in a bright, social tone. I realized what was happening. The woman upstairs—'Mrs Oxley,' Martin whispered in my ear—had come out to see what all the noise was. Carol was busy explaining to her who she was, was saying that Martin had got himself locked in, was asking if she had a key to the flat. Mrs Oxley sounded a bit suspicious.

Mrs Oxley then called out, 'Martin? Are you there, dear?'

He didn't answer. 'He's in there,' Carol said. 'He may have gone in another room.' She hammered on the door.

'She has a key,' Martin breathed in my ear.

He tugged at my sleeve and pointed to the back of the

flat. I saw what he meant. This was our chance to get out of the flat by the back door and away down the passage. Carol would convince Mrs Oxley in the end, adults always stick together. She might persuade her Martin must be hurt. She would produce her key in the end and come in. We had to be out. We took our coats off their hooks and went quietly down the passage to the kitchen. I unlocked the door and we went out and I closed it behind us. With luck they might not notice it was unlocked for a while.

17
Thursday afternoon
Martin

The garden was quite shadowy, and the shadows moved in the slight wind that had got up.

'Come on,' Hannah said. 'It'll get worse the more we wait.'

We edged to the corner of the house and looked round. The passage appeared to be clear to the front gate. I pulled the hood of my jacket up over my head, took a deep breath, and tip-toed up the path.

The worst bit was the corner by the front door, the obvious place for an ambush. I stood, poised to run but knowing there was nowhere to run to, and made myself look round. No one. Nothing. The door: quietly shut; the front garden: empty. I walked on, more confident now, to the front gate, still ready to run, to scream. I looked along the pavements, lit by the street lamps. They were empty. I beckoned sharply to Hannah and we turned out of the garden towards our bikes. As we went there was a knocking from Mrs Oxley's front window. I ignored it, didn't turn and look. She couldn't be sure it was me with my hood up, wouldn't know Hannah anyway. I started to run towards our bikes.

'We'd better go back to the boat,' Hannah said. 'There's nowhere else to go.'

I felt better once we were out of those quiet side roads and among the going-home people and the traffic. We cycled towards the canal, back to the boat, our last safe place. The tow-path was empty, and quite dark. The rain seemed stronger out here away from the houses. Perhaps it was actually just stronger. It turned into a hard, driving rain that quickly wet first my knees, then ran down into my trainers, and then seeped through my jacket. It was an effort to leave the bright and cheerful streets and go into that lurking empty dark with just our bicycle lights but somehow the misery of becoming wet made the dark easier to bear. We didn't talk, rode slowly and close together, so close that we bumped our wheels from time to time. Thank goodness we were on bikes so it didn't seem so far to the boat or I think my nerve would have cracked and I would have fled back to the lights. We stopped under a bridge to draw breath.

'What are we going to do?' I asked Hannah. 'We can't run and hide for ever.'

'We need your father,' she said. 'I keep telling you. We need him to sort it all out. He's the only person who can help.'

'Where on earth is he?' I said. I had a terrible fear that I couldn't put into words, not yet, not to Hannah, not even to myself, yet. I had gradually, over the last year or so, had to accept the fact, the bitter disappointing fact, that Dad was not a fighter. We had learnt in science that animals have two main defence mechanisms: flight and fight. Some animals run like mad when in danger, some turn and threaten. I remember going for a walk with Dad along the canal once. I must have been quite small. It was early summer and the canal was full of baby ducks. Then we came across the swan family. They were standing in the middle of the tow-path: mother, father, seven cygnets. Dad stopped. One swan turned its head slowly towards us. 'Let's just go through the bushes,' Dad said. We pushed our way through the bushes that grew alongside the tow-path until we were past the swans. I was scratched on my face and hands. When we got home Dad made a great dramatic story of it and said swans could break your legs with their wings. Mum just looked at him and laughed. I didn't understand then why she laughed. I still think Dad was right and that swans with their young are dangerous but I know now that Dad is one of nature's runners away. Mum is a fighter but he isn't. Perhaps he had run away now, wasn't able to cope with the threats.

'We'll have to wait for him,' Hannah said. 'He's bound to come back before long. We don't have a lot of choice. I can't think of any way out of this except telling your father, unless you want to go to the police.'

I shook my head. I was angry and hurt and confused, but I didn't want to sit in a police station telling my story. They probably wouldn't believe me anyway as Mum and The Man would deny it all, and what evidence did I have? And if they did believe me, would Mum go to prison? Did I want to send her to prison? Hannah was right: we had to find Dad, let him sort it out. He would believe me, he would without question, because he'd had the phone calls.

When we turned the last corner we saw the boat, glowing dimly on the water. Hannah braked instantly. 'There's someone there,' she whispered. We stood astride our bikes for a moment, staring in disbelief. Were they both sides of us?

'Come on,' she said, 'we have to know.'

We got off our bikes and leant them against the hedge, turned round ready to ride back. We walked softly along the grass edge until we reached the boat. It sat there in the water, looking harmless: door locked, windows shut. The cabin was lit up with its overhead bulb. We walked up and down getting bolder, peering in the windows. It seemed quite empty, quite undisturbed.

'Dad must have left the light on, in case we came back, to frighten us off. It's OK. Come on!'

I thought the boat was glowing less brightly. Perhaps it had seemed brighter at first because I had expected just a darker shape to tell us where it was. Then I heard Hannah cursing.

'He's let the battery run down,' she said. 'It needs to be on charge when the engine's on.' Even in the dim light that was coming through the open doorway she must have read in my face how I felt. 'Don't worry,' she said, 'we won't be in the dark all night. I'll get the candles out and then I'll put the lights out to rest the battery so we have enough charge to get the engine running, and then it will be fine. We'll move the boat in the morning. I couldn't do it in the dark and I don't want to sit here with the engine running; it'd be a dead give-away.'

18
Thursday, about 5.30 p.m.
Martin

We went into the kitchen and I stood there dripping miserably on to the floor while Hannah lit a couple of candles. She tipped them so that wax dripped on to a saucer and stuck them upright. When they were both well alight she switched the main cabin light off. I stood, still dripping, in the flickering shadows, cold, wet, utterly depressed. Hannah looked at me and laughed. The worse things got the more excited she seemed.

'Hey! The stove is gas; we can light that and get warmed up and dry.' She lit the little oven and left the door open and then lit both the gas rings on top. There was that sharp smell of bottled gas but I could immediately feel the heat coming out. I started to be able to move again and pulled my soaked jacket off and my trainers. My jeans were wet from the knees down but I wasn't going to take them off. Hannah rooted around in the drawers and found some string and used it to make a sort of washing line across the kitchen and hung our wet things up. I was still shivering, was in fact shivering more now, shivering great body-wrenching shakes, and she must have noticed because she went out and came back with a couple of duvets from the beds. I wrapped one round me and sat on the floor near the cooker and waited for the shaking to stop.

'Hot sweet tea is what we need,' she said, and filled the kettle and put it on the cooker. 'Watched kettles,' she said, and wandered out of the kitchen into the main cabin. A moment later I heard her say, 'Blow the candles out, quick!'

I pulled myself up and blew the candles out, too

dopey to argue. I was in a kind of dream where everything was happening very slowly and extra clearly. I felt the boat tip slightly, and tip again, and then lurch, and then the sound of the outer door closing and the key turning in the lock. I heard Hannah coming back across the cabin and into the kitchen. I looked at her. She was scared, really scared for the first time.

'They're coming along the tow-path,' she said, quietly, without inflection.

'Who are?' I asked stupidly, still in my unreal dream state. She didn't bother to answer me.

'He mustn't catch me with you. He mustn't catch me. Why ever did I help you? I knew I shouldn't. He'll kill me.'

'But you said I'd kidnapped you,' I said, stupidly, forgetting everything that had happened in her house. 'He can't think it's your fault.'

'He can't find me!' she moaned. 'He can't find me!'

'He won't do anything to you, surely?'

'You don't know him. He loses his temper. He does things then. That's why Mum left.'

'Can't we move the boat?' I asked.

'The engine wouldn't start. I don't want to be outside. He'll get me if I'm outside. I untied it. That's all I had time for. They were close. I heard them.'

And then I heard, too. The Man's voice, firm, clear, just outside. 'Come out, you two, now. The game's over. You're not going anywhere. Come on, we're all going home.'

'We'd better do what he says,' I said.

'No, please, you don't know him,' Hannah moaned again, sinking to the floor. 'Please, Martin, don't open the door. Please.'

I took the two steps across to the window and looked cautiously out. There was a torch shining on to the boat and in its light I could see that we had drifted a little way from the bank. I really didn't know what to do. If we didn't open the door, would he be able to knock it in? And wouldn't having to damage his beloved boat make him even angrier? We couldn't start the engine without going out. We couldn't escape anywhere unless the boat drifted over to the other bank, and even then, where could we go?

Hannah was still moaning on the floor. This was so unlike her and I realized suddenly how she had made all the decisions, had kept me going and now she couldn't cope at all, couldn't meet her father face to face and stand up to him, out of fear. I didn't think I could betray her after all she had done for me. We had no way out, there was no way out, but I wasn't going to give myself up, give her up to him. It's my life, I kept muttering, it's my life.

There was more shouting from outside, from further away this time, and then there was a tremendous lurch of the boat and Hannah screamed and a face was at the window, staring in, filling the glass. Eyes and mouth, wide open. Coming to get me. To get us. About to break through. Coming, coming . . .

I leaped back, back as far as I could go, away from the face, the eyes, the mouth. I could not move far. Something was behind my back but I pressed myself as far from the window as I could. I felt the heat of the stove, felt it getting hotter, heard The Man hammering on the side of the boat, shouting out of that great mouth, saw Hannah on the floor staring at me in horror, heard her screaming, 'Martin! Martin!' and at that moment felt flames leap on to my hair.

Hannah was on her feet and pulling the flaming duvet off me and swiping at my head and trying to wrap her coat round me and I was screaming too and the face at the window had gone silent and was staring in horror as the flames stretched towards us. The duvet writhed as it burnt and the carpet under it was alight and the line of our clothes dripped fire. For a moment it was all beautiful: red, orange, tongues licking greedily, upwards, downwards, always towards us, the heat of hell with the devil mouthing outside.

Hannah pulled at me, shouting: 'Out! We've got to get out!' Smoke was filling the kitchen now, black smothering smoke that hid the flames. We stumbled towards the cabin, crashed through the doorway. The smoke rushed after us, determined to confuse us, to choke us, to suck us into its red heart.

We were choking, retching, staggering.

'Down!' I shouted, and as I shouted fresh smoke filled my lungs and I coughed and coughed and croaked out: 'Down below the smoke!'

'Out!' Hannah yelled, coughed. 'The door!'

But where was the door? There was no door, no Hannah, no anything, just the smoke. I tried to drop to the floor but something was stopping me. A hand.

The hand tugged at me, tugged at me. Suddenly there was the door, the locked door. I could hear Hannah struggle with the key, hear it rattle endlessly, but I could see nothing. Then the hand tugged at me again and I moved forward in the smoke and we were out into the air, a sudden coldness and Hannah straight in front of me. I dragged in a breath, a desperate lunge at the air outside, air that was being poisoned rapidly by the smoke that was rushing after us. There were voices shouting all round. Shapes of people lit up in the hell fire danced and waved on the bank and on the boat the devil himself was shouting something and edging towards us.

'The gas!' Hannah was screaming in my face. 'The gas!' And her cry seemed to be her father's cry and it was taken up by the figures on the bank and the smoky air was filled with 'Gas! Gas!'

I couldn't think what she meant, what they all meant. She was tugging and tugging at me but there was nowhere to go. Water was all round us, the black foul canal water, looking almost solid in the darkness. The bank was too far away to jump, and too full of enemies. I stood on the end of the boat. Flames were now following the smoke out of the door and I tried to stand away from them, but Hannah was pulling at me, pulling desperately, desperately, even though there was nowhere to go, and I began to lose my balance and grabbed at her to steady myself but she was pulling at me still and I felt us both falling . . .

. . . and as we fell the whole world exploded.

19
Thursday, perhaps 7 p.m.
Martin

The canal closed over our heads as the boat exploded. I was suddenly very cold. My mouth filled with water and my feet sank into soft, clinging mud. I struggled and kicked and my head came out into the air as the blazing boat scattered itself all around. Hannah's head was next to me. We seemed to be in the centre of cascading fire that sizzled on the water.

One of the figures on the tow-path had jumped into the canal and was half swimming, half wading towards us. Dad. He grabbed me and Hannah and pulled us to the bank. There was no danger of us drowning really as the canal was too shallow but we were dazed and confused, and becoming very cold.

Bits of burning boat floating on the water and on the banks lit up the scene like a Guy Fawkes evening. Dad had brought us to the opposite bank from the others, I don't know whether by accident, and we all stood there staring across at each other. Two of them, three of us. The Man, Hannah's father, John Woodbridge, had jumped clear just before the fire had shattered the kitchen window where he stood. His leap was burnt into my memory. It seemed out of time. It looked as though he had been thrown by the explosion, but that had come after and I thought stupidly it was like the gap between lightning and thunder, but I realized later he had known the boat would explode and had jumped just before it did. He had been shouting at us to jump, shouting about the gas cylinder. He and Mum had burnt clothes, singed hair.

'Are you all right?' Mum shouted.

'A lot you care,' Dad shouted back.

We all stood, glaring across the burning water. The flames started to die down and the darkness began to close in. Dad still had his arm on me and I leant against him. 'You OK?' he asked softly. I nodded, shaking.

'We need to talk about this,' Mr Woodbridge shouted. 'Sort things out.'

'Tomorrow,' Dad said. 'I'm taking them back with me and you'll stay away. You come near and I'll ring the police. I may do it anyway. We'll see. But one more move from you and it's 999.'

'You can't take my daughter,' Mr Woodbridge shouted.

Dad looked at Hannah, and I looked too. 'Daughter?' he said scornfully. 'Do you really care what happens to her? What do you want?' he asked her. 'It's up to you. Come with Martin and me tonight or go back with him?'

'I'm coming with you,' she said.

'Did you hear that?' Dad said, not shouting but speaking slowly and clearly. There wasn't any need to shout. The canal wasn't that wide but Mr Woodbridge was in a temper and shouted from rage and frustration. His plan was thwarted, his boat blown to pieces, his daughter disowned him. Mum just stood there.

'We're going now,' Dad said. 'I'll ring you tomorrow to arrange a meeting. We'll sort everything out then. Remember, I'll ring the police if you do anything at all, anything.'

We walked along the canal bank towards the bridge. The ground was rough and I staggered and stumbled and would have fallen if Dad hadn't been holding my arm. He held Hannah on the other side. We were soon in darkness and seemed to be walking for ever. I was soaked through and shivering again. 'Nearly there,' Dad kept saying. 'Just keep going. Nearly there.'

And then we were there, clambering up from the field on to the road and there was Dad's car parked and we were sitting in it and he was driving us back to his flat.

'My bike,' I said.

Dad laughed.

After laughing about my bike Dad said nothing more until we got back to his flat. He parked outside and I saw Mrs Oxley's curtain pulled back and her face at the window. Before we had walked as far as the front door she had opened it and was coming down the path towards us.

'You're soaking wet!' she said, almost as if we were naughty children who had been playing in their best clothes.

'It's a long story,' Dad said. 'I think they just need a hot drink and bed.'

'I'll decide about that,' she said. 'They may well need to go to Casualty.'

She fussed us up the stairs to her flat. 'I've got the kettle on all ready. And Hannah can stay in my spare room. The bed's all made up. I always keep it ready, just in case. It's all aired.' It was typical that she knew Hannah's name already, must have picked it up from Mum and put it away in her efficient filing-cabinet memory. It didn't seem any time at all before Dad and I had been given a drink and shooed out of the flat and sent on our way downstairs. Dad put me in his bed and said he'd sleep on the sofa, 'fitting punishment' he called it. I was too tired to argue and went straight to sleep and slept soundly. The nightmares didn't start till later. I just felt it was all over at last. It wasn't, of course. Nothing ever is.

20
Now
Martin

In my nightmares now there are always three parts. They don't always come in the same order and they twine in and out of each other in new and frightening combinations. When I sit up in bed, shaking and sweating, looking about my room reassuring myself, it's just a dream, just a dream, I find it helps to disentangle them, lay them out and stare them in the face until they fade. The trouble with dreams is, they happen so slowly. When the boat really blew up it was so quick I didn't know what had happened but my treacherous memory stored every detail and brings them out to torture me at night. Let me lay them out now, in proper chronological order, and as my dreams remember, not what I took in at the time, and let me try to exorcise the fear by calm analysis.

Three parts, then. In reality, over in seconds. In dreams, played out at night so unbearably slowly.

First, the explosion. I know now that the fire in the kitchen had heated the gas cylinder beyond its safety limit and it had exploded in that little space. The immediate sensation in that micro second when Hannah and I were falling together off the boat was a blinding whiteness which lit the world so brightly that shapes were black holes. Two figures now on the tow-path, black shapes like blasted trees in a lightning flash, one bending away, arms up to protect invisible faces, the other reaching hopeless hands towards me. The shape that had leapt off the boat just before the explosion now lay sprawled on the bank.

And although I am already falling, the whole air collapses together and pushes me with its giant's fist.

The second part of the nightmare, which sometimes comes first, or, worse, last as if this is how it might all have ended, is cold, black, silent, still. I have so often dived into the swimming pool and know how quickly the water pushes you out again, and yet in the nightmare the water swallows me, cradles me so that I have time to see the underwater world of the canal. It is vast and black, and yet I can see. I can see the debris of ages, the cast off, thrown out, mostly of my own life, my toys, my bike, my whole bedroom, all lie half buried in the seething mud. Livid green and slimy tendrils snake towards me to entwine my legs, my arms, to swathe my face. And creatures ring me, gloating.

I drift, soundlessly slow-motioning through the blackness, already drowned.

The last part is the strangest because I am looking at myself, or rather, looking at my head. Just my head, because the rest of me doesn't seem to exist any more. My mouth is wide, straining, my eyes wide, glinting. My head is circled by fire, islands of fire like miniature erupting volcanoes. I know when I am awake that I am looking at the flat black surface of the canal, that I am standing on the muddy bottom so that my head is above water, that bits of burning boat are floating all around me, spluttering on contact with the water. When I am asleep, in the nightmare, my head is on this black plain surrounded by fire and I am watching it.

These three twist in and out of each other. Often there is a long sequence before they appear but I know they are coming, closer, closer, and I am drowned or vaporized or just a watching head and I struggle to wake . . .

21
Friday morning
Hannah

Next morning was explanations, after we had all woken late, after we had all had breakfast, after Martin's dad, Robert, had extracted me from Mrs Oxley whose curiosity was making her so restless she couldn't sit still for a moment. She had been very kind, but she couldn't bear not to know and I couldn't bear to tell her. Robert dealt with her by asking her if she could cook lunch for us and that sent her rushing out to shop.

We sat round the table in the window downstairs, all formal and tongue-tied to start with. I felt half-asleep still and embarrassed and worried. I couldn't stay with Mrs Oxley for ever, didn't want to even, certainly didn't want to go home but didn't see what alternative there was. Robert kept saying wet things like, 'Difficult to know where to begin, I suppose.' I suppose I was still dog tired. I know I slept a lot over the next few days, kept nodding off any time I sat down. Martin just sat at first, but I could see he was getting worked up, quite angry.

'Why didn't you tell me you'd won the lottery?' he burst out, interrupting Robert's ramblings.

Robert laughed. That really annoyed me. The whole awful experience we had been through, caused by his lottery win, and all he could do was laugh. It seemed to be the last straw for Martin.

'Why?' he shouted. I was embarrassed for him because I could feel he was about to burst into tears.

'We've a right to know,' I said.

He looked at me and stopped laughing. 'I'm in this syndicate at work,' he said. 'There are five of us. We club together and buy a few tickets each week. We did win. We won ten pounds.' I stared. Ten pounds? All this for ten pounds? I didn't believe it. 'I suppose it's my fault,' he went on. 'We thought it was such a joke, two pounds each. We went out to the pub at lunch time and blew it all in one round of drinks. We made a great thing about how we'd won the lottery and walked out of work, you know. It was funny at the time. Strangers coming up and congratulating us. We never said how much it was. That was the point of the whole thing. Though I suppose we did go on about spending huge amounts of money, as if we had won a lot.'

'Which pub?' I asked.

'The Foresters in Bosham Road. Why?'

'That's where my father drinks sometimes.'

'Next thing was, I got a phone call, Martin. Your mother. To tell me you had been kidnapped. She sounded strange somehow. I know now that she was acting; she never was much good at pretending. At the time something just niggled at me. I was terrified at first and then, for some reason, I got suspicious. I didn't think about the lottery win; it was just a joke, not real. No one in their right mind would think I'd got the amount of money they were asking for. So I drove round to the house.

'I stood outside on the pavement,' he went on, 'in the dark and could see in. Carol was watching TV, and laughing. So I began to think something odd was going on. She certainly wasn't worried so why should I be? I went home and the next thing was your phone call. I have to say I thought then it was you, Martin, just having a joke. Then I thought it just wasn't like you, and the instructions under the dustbin, they weren't like you, so I was worried, but not that worried.

'I sat and thought about it and decided the only thing was to go along with it, see what happened. I didn't want to go to the police in case it was just some elaborate joke. I thought it really had to be a joke; it wasn't real. So, next morning I drove to the phone box, as instructed, and just kept saying there wasn't any money until the phone went dead. Then I came home. I was getting a bit fed up with it by this stage, I can tell you. I thought that the best way of stopping it all was if I wasn't around so I went up to Mrs Oxley and told her some story about family problems and lawyers and stayed in her flat. I rang in to the office and said I wouldn't be in as I had someone to see, but left it vague and stayed in the flat all day. I saw you going out of the gate and I banged on the window but you didn't look up.'

'How did you find us?' I asked. Martin looked too shaken by might-have-beens to think. If onlys were filling my mind, and they must have been filling his too.

'You might call it luck but it wasn't that surprising. I saw which way you went, rushed down and drove after you. Luckily, Mrs Oxley had taken your mother into my flat and I got past them unseen. I thought I'd just watch where you went first. I lost you when you went down to the tow-path. I thought at first you'd gone into a house and just hung about not knowing what to do but then this other car drove up in a hurry and Carol and a man got out and I saw where they went and followed them, from a safe distance. The rest you know.'

We sat, all feeling a bit down, a bit limp after all the excitement. I couldn't see what was going to happen next, how we got out of all this.

22
Friday afternoon
Martin

We had lunch early. Dad told us he'd rung Mum and arranged to meet to sort everything out. He seemed to think we'd be coming with him.

'I'm not coming,' I said. I had decided this morning that I was going to take charge of my own life. I couldn't trust anyone else. Everyone had let me down.

'It's no good running away from things, Martin,' Dad said. I thought that was good, coming from him, but I didn't say it—luckily, because he went on. 'I know. I've run away from enough things and it doesn't solve them. Better face this, together.'

'He's not ready yet,' Mrs Oxley said. 'You're asking too much, Robert.'

'I'll come with you if you want, Martin,' Hannah said.

I looked at her. She was pale and exhausted. I was suddenly ashamed of thinking that she had let me down. She'd fought as hard as she could, rescued me, saved my life on the boat. She'd weakened when face-to-face with her father, but she hadn't given in. And she was still prepared to go on. Right, I was going to be in charge, but I could certainly do with some help.

'Your father will be there,' Dad said.

She swallowed. 'I'll come if Martin does.'

They all looked at me. 'OK,' I said.

Hannah was looking pretty gloomy all through lunch. 'Tell me about your mother,' Dad said to her.

To my embarrassment she started crying. 'I'll do a bit of washing up,' I said and took things out to the kitchen and clattered away in the sink. I thought she might be happier talking to Dad without me listening. There wasn't anything I could do to help anyway.

Mrs Oxley came out and we talked about the house. It seemed Dad had already been working things out. What I didn't know before was that Mrs Oxley owned the whole house; it used to be her family home and when her husband died she had it converted into flats so that she could stay there and also get some income from it. Apparently, the people in the top flat were leaving after Easter. It was another two-bedroom flat and Dad could have it and I could live with him. Until Easter I could use the spare room in Mrs Oxley's flat, if I could be clean, tidy, and quiet. How did I feel about this?

There was no doubt about how I felt. It's awful to say you like one parent more than the other, but it's true in my case. Dad was always easier, more considerate, more interested. I could certainly put up with Mrs Oxley's kind nosiness for a few months, especially now I couldn't stand the thought of going home.

After a bit Hannah came out and suggested we went to collect our bikes as we had a couple of hours before the meeting. She was a bit pink-eyed but seemed more cheerful. She said Dad had some more phone calls to make and would rather do them without us there. Our trainers were still a bit damp but Mrs Oxley had put everything through the washer and drier so we could go out looking normal, whatever we felt like inside. The rain had passed over and it was a crisp, sunny afternoon.

Our bikes were still leaning against the hedge where we had left them, looking just the same. Nothing else did. The tow-path had little pieces of charred wood on it and the grass verge had burnt patches. Worst was the canal itself which now looked like something out of a horror film. Canal water is always an unhealthy-looking green, like the surface of some alien planet. Sticking out was this great black mouth: the blackened edge of the hull of the boat. Little bits of black floated randomly.

We stood and looked at it, the sunshine glinting on the water. I thought how nearly I was trapped inside the cabin, how nearly I too was charred remains. It didn't seem real this afternoon.

'Serves him right,' Hannah said.

We turned away and got on our bikes and rode back to the town. We met two British Waterways workmen who asked if we'd seen a wrecked boat. We pointed back the way we'd come. The work of clearing up and sorting out had started.

23
Friday, early evening
Martin

It was awful. Almost the worst thing of all. Walking back into 'home'. Facing Mum. Sitting down, all of us.

But I did it. Dad was right. I felt better after for having faced her. Hannah sat beside me. It must have been as bad for her. Worse. I had Dad. She had nobody. I was going home with Dad when all this was over. Where had she to go, except back with her father? I hadn't thought of her having to go and live with The Man, and perhaps my mother. They might well think it was all her fault, especially the boat being blown up. She'd said her father was very keen on his boat and now there was nothing left of it at all. Things could be very tense in her house, and she'd also said he'd got a very bad temper, and Mum wasn't one to miss an opportunity to remind someone of what they'd done wrong, on a regular basis, like several times a day.

The best thing was, Mrs Oxley was there too. I was surprised at first but I think it wouldn't have worked without her. There'd have been rows and a fight, probably. She took over and just said what was going to happen. She and Dad seemed to have it all worked out. Mum sat in silence. Hannah's dad kept trying to say things but she wouldn't let him.

She let Mum ask me the question I'd been dreading. I could say what I wanted when she wasn't there, but to her face? 'What about you, Martin?' Mum asked me. 'I'm really sorry about everything that's happened and I'd like you to come home.'

I managed to look at her. I think she was sorry (though I noticed she didn't actually say she was sorry for what she had done, only for 'everything that's happened' as if it wasn't actually her fault) but I wasn't coming 'home'. 'No,' I said. 'I'm staying with Dad.' She dropped her eyes first. Somehow I didn't feel like someone who's just won a great victory.

'. . . and Hannah will come back with me for the moment until something else can be worked out,' Mrs Oxley was saying when he erupted.

'No she isn't!' he shouted, on his feet now, red in the face. I felt Hannah shrink down next to me on the sofa, trembling. 'Listen, you interfering, bossy old bat, she's coming home with me, and we're going now!'

Mrs Oxley didn't stir. 'Sit down, Mr Woodbridge,' she said, icy, and to my surprise he did.

'I may be bossy, and old, and perhaps a bat,' she said, 'but I am not interfering. I am here at Robert's invitation. I was a doctor before I retired and I know exactly what my legal duty is. I know exactly who to telephone and I know exactly what will happen if I do. Hannah will be taken into care. You will be charged with abduction. The children will have to give evidence. The tabloids will be in full cry. I'm sure none of you want all that to happen.'

'No,' Mum said, very quietly.

'What we are trying to work out is something better for the children, something they can accept and that will help them to get over this terrible thing you have done to them,' Mrs Oxley went on. 'They should be our main concern after all. We will ask Hannah what she wants. Hannah, would you prefer to go with your father now, in which case I have to tell you I shall almost certainly feel I have to report him, or would you rather come back with me?'

Hannah was crying. It didn't help me. I was nearly crying too. 'With you,' she managed to say. Her father thumped the arm of his chair but said nothing.

Mrs Oxley sent me and Hannah upstairs to collect some of my clothes. The voices went on.

24
Now
Martin

Time passed, hours first and then days, and weeks, and Dad's plans seemed to work like magic, helped by luck. I suddenly realized that he was quite efficient, quite business-like, and then wondered why I was surprised. I suppose Mum had always been the organizer at home, been at home more, and Dad had just gone along with things. Perhaps that's what caused the trouble between them.

Hannah's father and my mum broke up and he moved away to find another job. Her mother came back—Dad had tracked her down—and she sold their large house and she and Hannah now live near us. Hannah left her private school and came to mine. Dad and I moved into the top flat. He insists that I go to see Mum once a week. I don't stop or have a meal or anything but just call in for an embarrassing half hour on Saturday mornings. Dad says it will get better if I keep at it. It hasn't, yet.

It wasn't until early summer that I went back along the tow-path. Hannah came with me. There was no sign that anything had happened. Grass had grown back and the debris had gone. The water of the canal lay untroubled, hiding everything in its murky depths. We looked for a moment and then cycled on. Nothing seemed to have changed, but everything had.

Other Oxford books by Michael Harrison

Junk Mail

ISBN 0 19 276113 7

In his first collection of original poems, Michael Harrison writes about haircuts, dead ends, hating teachers, walking to the moon, the end of the world, and how to recognize rude words.

There are also various pieces of junk mail to Miss Muffet (from the Rent-a-Spider Company), to Prince Charming (from the Fitter Foot Firm), and to Humpty Dumpty (from the Wallsend China Company). There's also a poem to a real junk male.

'a provocative mix of funny, thoughtful, lyrical poems.'
Michael Rosen in *The Guardian*

Don Quixote

ISBN 0 19 274165 9

Illustrated by Victor G Ambrus

He lived in a small village in a dusty corner of Spain, a bony man of about 50. He had little to do, and so he read. About the knights of old who roamed the countryside seeking adventures. He knew that he too must be a knight, travel on a quest, must seek adventures. So he found a suit of rusty armour, made a visor of cardboard and tin, and called himself Don Quixote de la Mancha.

This is a spirited retelling of the famous novel by Miguel de Cervantes Saavedra. Michael Harrison's clear and lively style is complemented by Victor Ambrus's evocative paintings of sixteenth-century Spain.

'This is a beautiful book which would find a very special place on any bookshelf, to be enjoyed by child, parent and grandparent alike.'
Spoken English